Escape from
Fire Lake

Escape *from* Fire Lake

Robert Vernon

Based on the story and characters
created by Robert Vernon
and the screenplay by Pete Lynch Tobin
and Stephen Stiles

Tyndale House Publishers, Inc.
WHEATON, ILLINOIS

The Last Chance Detectives and *The Last Chance Detectives* logo are
trademarks of Focus on the Family.

Scripture quotations, except page 67, are taken from the *Holy Bible,* New
International Version®. Copyright © 1973, 1978, 1984 by International Bible
Society. Used by permission of Zondervan Publishing House. All rights reserved.
The "NIV" and "New International Version" trademarks are registered in the United
States Patent and Trademark Office by International Bible Society. Use of either
trademark requires permission of International Bible Society.

The Scripture quotation on page 67 is taken from the *Holy Bible,* King James Version.

Library of Congress Cataloging-in-Publication Data

Vernon, Robert, date
    Escape from Fire Lake / Robert Vernon.
        p. cm. — (The Last Chance Detectives ; 3)
    "Based on the story and characters created by Robert Vernon and the screen-
play by Pete Lynch Tobin and Stephen Stiles."
    Summary: When bank robbers hit Ambrosia, Arizona, twelve-year-old Mike
stumbles onto their trail and finds himself kidnapped, only to be turned loose in
the desert, while the other Last Chance Detectives search for their leader.
    ISBN 0-8423-2062-8
    [1. Mystery and detective stories.   2. Arizona—Fiction.]   I. Title.   II. Series.
PZ7.V5983Es   1996
[Fic]—dc20   96-3720

Printed in the United States of America

02   01   00   99   98   97   96
 9   8   7   6   5   4   3   2

To my father—
A man of integrity who
gave me my love for
storytelling

No one noticed when two men in a 1971 Cadillac pulled into the small town of Ambrosia and cruised down Main Street. Not that anyone should. Being located next to historic Route 66 meant that a constant flow of cars and their road-weary passengers stopped by to make one last pit stop before braving the next hundred or so miles of blistering desert. The car looked like just another asphalt-eating sedan with the typical layer of fine red dust and a windshield spattered with a diverse collection of unlucky bugs.

There was really only one thing unique about this car. It was stolen.

Josh Pendleton was a strongly built man. He had added pounds of muscle to his wide frame by spending many hours pumping weights in the prison yard. He held the Cadillac's steering wheel in a steel grip as he turned the car from Main Street onto First. He brushed his dark hair out of his eyes and kept an eye on the speedometer to make sure he didn't exceed the speed limit. He had planned things too well to be caught now by some small-town traffic cop with a radar gun. The bank was just a few blocks ahead.

Seth Parker sat next to him and peered out from under his cowboy hat. Beads of sweat leaked out from under the hatband as his tongue nervously played with a toothpick in his mouth. No matter how hard he tried to relax, he didn't think that he'd ever get used to the nerve-racking moments just before a job.

This would be their third bank robbery in two weeks. The other two had been in small towns as well. But they had been really nothing more than practice runs preparing them for this—their grab at the big brass ring in the bank of Ambrosia.

They had met in Huntsville Penitentiary. Josh considered crime his profession, while Seth was only serving a short sentence for some petty thefts. Seth had just wanted to quietly do his time and then go home. But then Josh schemed up this plan, and when Seth heard how easy it would be and how rich it would make them both—he just couldn't pass it up.

Josh had always been the mastermind, planning each job he and his accomplices pulled off. But this job practically landed right in his lap. He had been assigned to work in the prison hospital when a dying convict told him a wild tale about a priceless jade statuette dating back to the Ming dynasty. The old man had been part of a ring of professional thieves who had smuggled it out of the Orient. Although it was worth hundreds of thousands of dollars, the smugglers decided that they had better not try to sell it until things cooled off on the black market. So they hid it in a place where they thought no one would ever track it: a safety-deposit box in the small town of Ambrosia. The old man just had to get the story off his chest before he went to meet his Maker. He told Josh to tell the warden so the rightful owners could reclaim it.

But Josh had other ideas.

It wasn't hard to figure out which bank it was

in. Ambrosia just had two, and only one offered safety-deposit boxes.

The plan was simple: Get in and out of the bank as fast as possible, make a clean getaway in the stolen car, and drive a few blocks to a waiting truck in a secluded spot. By the time the police had a description of the getaway car, Josh and Seth would be driving out of town in a clean vehicle. Easy as pie.

Josh eased the Caddy over to the curb and turned off the ignition.

"Kind of a small bank, isn't it?" drawled Seth in a thick Texas accent as he peered out the windshield.

"That's what makes it so perfect," Josh said with a smile. He reached into the backseat to retrieve a duffel bag, and then he checked his watch. "OK. The vault should be open. We've got five minutes . . . so keep your eyes peeled for the grand prize."

From behind the sun visor, Josh produced a neatly creased paper and unfolded it for Seth to see. "Take a good look. This is what's gonna make it all worthwhile."

The paper was a Xerox copy of a drawing of the statuette. It didn't look like much to Seth—a glaring panther head set atop a long body, enshrouded in two hawkish wings. Seth wondered what rich people saw in trinkets such as this. His appreciation of the fine arts extended only about as far as his collection of velvet Elvis pictures.

"What if it's not here?" Seth asked as he checked his own duffel bag one last time.

"Oh, it's here." Josh replied firmly. "Stolen goods like to hide out in dusty little towns like this. I did my homework."

Seth smiled and shook his head in admiration. "You're somethin', Josh. Now we take it from the first guys that stole it."

Josh pulled a revolver from his bag and twirled it nimbly in his palm before tucking it down into the waist of his pants. The ease and skill with which he used it worried Seth.

"Don't worry! No one's gonna get hurt!" Josh assured him. "Now remember, I'll take care of the safety-deposit boxes. You keep everyone covered and empty the cash tills. That way we'll have a few bucks for spending cash. You ready?"

Josh is right, thought Seth. *A small-town bank like this probably won't even have a guard.* He grabbed his bag and looked firmly into Josh's eyes. "Yeah, I'm ready!"

"Good," Josh said with a slight laugh in his voice. "Then it's time to make a little 'withdrawal'!"

As the two men exited the car and walked up to the bank, they took one last look around. Aside from the usual passing cars, the street looked quiet. They politely opened the door for an exiting patron, then stepped into the bank.

🌵

Mike Fowler knew the streets of Ambrosia like the back of his hand. He had moved here with his mother to live with his grandparents after the "accident." His father had been flying a secret mission over a hot spot in the Middle East when his plane went down. Although the military had never found his body, they had no reason to believe he had escaped and had assumed he died in the crash.

But Mike didn't think so. He knew his dad was a fighter and would have found some way to survive. The very fact that no one had found a body or any dog tags was proof enough. To Mike it wasn't just a hope, it was a fact: His father was alive somewhere. He could feel it. Probably being held captive by some terrorist organization. And although almost everyone else had given up hope, he hadn't. And he intended to prove them wrong someday. But being twelve years old meant that he couldn't do much for the time being.

Mike's dad had always told him that he could

accomplish almost anything he wanted to as long as he really set his mind to it. Combine that with a little practice and a lot of hard work, and almost any obstacle could be scaled. So with that in mind, Mike figured that if he was ever going to solve the mystery of what happened to his dad, he'd better start practicing now. That's how he came up with the idea for the Last Chance Detectives.

Mike named the group after the diner that his family ran at the edge of town: the Last Chance Diner and Gas Station. His grandfather, Pop Fowler, let Mike use his old B-17 bomber as the headquarters. Then Mike had recruited the help of his three best friends, Ben Jones, Wynona Whitefeather, and Spencer Martin. And so far they had a pretty good track record. Whether it was investigating strange UFO lights out in the desert or trailing the legendary bigfoot, the Last Chance Detectives always solved their case.

They only had one problem: finding good mysteries to solve.

Not much happens in a small town, so the biggest challenge for Mike—since the task usually fell to him—was to find interesting cases that would hone their detective skills.

And that's exactly what Mike had on his mind the morning of the bank robbery.

He and the gang were coming up a side street

less than a block away from the bank when the robbers first entered the building. They were on their way home from an early morning baseball game and engaging in one of their favorite pastimes—sports trivia. Mike threw a ball for his dog, Jake, to retrieve as he tried to think up a question to stump them.

"Spence!" Mike called out. "Longest home run."

Spence didn't even miss a beat. "Mickey Mantle, 643 feet, 1960!"

Mike threw his arms up. There was no tripping up Spence. The guy was a walking encyclopedia. "Your turn, Winnie," Mike said with a sigh.

"Ben!" Winnie challenged. "Most steals in a season."

"Um . . . give me a second! I know this one." Ben stalled, his face contorted in deep concentration.

Just to add a little pressure, Winnie started humming the theme music to *Jeopardy.* She knew this bugged him.

"Um, Lou Brock!" Ben exclaimed in triumph.

"Brrrnk!" Winnie made the sound of a game-show buzzer.

Winnie, Mike, and Spence all knew the answer to this one, and they chimed in unison, "Ricky Henderson, 130 for Oakland, 1982."

Ben grimaced as the other three laughed.

The robbery was going exactly as planned. Seth had already emptied the cash drawers, and Josh was going through the safety-deposit boxes one by one with a master key. The bank clerks and by-standers had given up without a fuss and now lay flat on the cracked tile floor. Seth kept watch over them, pacing back and forth, cradling a sawed-off shotgun in his arms.

Seth felt a weird surge of emotions as he waited for Josh to finish the job. On the one hand, an adrenaline rush made him feel strangely powerful. On the other, he couldn't turn off the voice that kept repeating the words *This is wrong!*

As he looked down at the trembling victims, his heart couldn't help but feel sorry for them. He wasn't like Josh. Josh had done this type of thing too many times to have his conscience bother him. Seth wondered if he, too, might eventually become as calloused. If this job panned out as well as they hoped, he wouldn't have to. He looked at his watch. In just a few minutes, this would all be a thing of the past. In just a few min-utes, he and Josh would be rich men. In just a few minutes—

Catching a glimpse of movement in the corner of his eye, Seth's head snapped to look across the room. Just outside the window, four kids and a dog emerged from around the corner. If they glanced into the bank, they would easily see what was going on! Seth held his breath and hoped they would continue on by.

They didn't. They paused to stop and talk.

Seth tried not to panic as he racked his brain as to what he should do. The venetian blinds! If he could maneuver across the room and close the blinds . . .

The Last Chance Detectives rounded the corner and stopped in front of the bank. Mike, Ben, and Winnie gathered with their backs to the bank window. Spence stood facing them with a clear view into the bank.

"OK, this is where we split up and start looking," said Mike. "Here's the plan—"

"Il-li-nois!" Ben interrupted, hitting Spence in the arm once for every syllable. It was just another ongoing game he and Spence played. The basic rule was this: Whoever saw an out-of-state license plate first got to sock the other guy in the arm.

"Where?" cried Spence, looking around and holding his arm in pain.

Ben pointed just a few yards away to the 1971 Cadillac parked at the curb. "I get you every time, Spence," Ben laughed. "You oughta be wearing your glasses."

"I can see fine without my glasses," Spence replied defensively as he turned back to face the bank again.

"Cool it, Ben," Mike said, trying to bring some order to the day. "It's time for business. OK, here's the deal—we split up, look for anything worth investigating, and meet back at the B-17 at five-thirty. We'll vote on the best case. Questions?"

Spence squinted his eyes as he noticed some movement in the bank. Try as he might, he couldn't bring it into focus. He realized that Ben was probably right—he should be wearing his glasses. All he could make out in the bank were blurs of motion.

"How can we choose a case when there's nothing going on?" Ben asked, looking at the others. "Hasn't been for weeks."

Ben noticed Spence's eyes squinting and turned to see what he was trying to focus on. The miniblinds closed with a snap.

"He's got a point," Winnie noted.

"That was yesterday. Today is going to be our day!" said Mike, trying to encourage the others. He took a deep breath through his nose. "Smell that? That's a case. A good detective can always smell a case."

Winnie, Ben, and Spence each sniffed the air. Winnie suddenly got a disgusted look on her face.

"I think those are Ben's socks."

"Ha-ha," said Ben dryly.

"OK, you've got till five-thirty," said Mike, ignoring the last two comments. "Keep your eyes open."

With a couple of parting waves, the kids went their separate ways, not knowing how close they had come to their next case.

2

The Howdy Partner! Motor Lodge had been something when it first opened in the late '40s. In those days, the motel was ideal. Located on the edge of town, it had forty adobe rooms—complete with hot and cold running taps—surrounding a sparkling horseshoe-shaped pool. Out front, a twenty-foot-tall neon cowboy continuously twirled his rope as he invited motorists to stop on in and rest a spell. With a seemingly endless stream of customers, the No Vacancy sign buzzed to life almost every night.

But in the early '70s the great interstate freeway went in, bypassing Ambrosia by over fifty miles. As motorists opted to stay on the large eight-lane superhighway, the steady stream of traffic slowed to a trickle. And the Howdy Partner! began to die.

In the late '80s a renewed interest in the American experience was born. Baby boomers who warmly remembered the long trips with their parents down historic Route 66 hit the road in search of their golden memories. Nostalgia had found Ambrosia, and the town was experiencing its second boom of business.

But it was too late for the Howdy Partner! It had closed its doors for good in 1975. It now stood a vacant shell, a shadow of what it had been in its glory days. The windows and doors were boarded over. The paint was faded and peeling from countless hours in the sun. The sparkling pool was filled in with cement. The neon cowboy hung precariously off his stand, his neon tubing long ago broken by vandals. A dilapidated fence now surrounded the property, but it, too, was starting to give in to the strong winds that blew in off the desert. Large sections had fallen over, and on the sections that did survive, official-look-ing signs warned trespassers that the property had been condemned.

Occasionally a tourist would venture past the fence, snapping a Polaroid for his scrapbook back home. Other than that, no one came around the motor lodge anymore. And that's exactly why Josh Pendleton had chosen it.

Within the seclusion of the courtyard, Seth Parker emptied the stolen Cadillac of the last two money bags he needed to transfer. Josh was busy in the back of a World War II—era troop trans-port. It was a large green army truck, with a can-vas canopy over the back. It wasn't a very common truck to see on the road, but Josh wasn't worried if it attracted a little attention. He had paid cash for it back in New Mexico, and if the cops ran the plates, it would come up clean.

As Seth neared the truck, Josh reached into the back and pulled out an expensive-looking foot-long teak box. He gingerly unsnapped a small brass hook on its side and opened it wide for Seth to see. "Feast your eyes, Seth. This is gonna fatten up our wallets big time."

The statuette was smaller than Seth had thought it would be. But it was also much more beautiful. Although only about a foot tall, the intricate detailed carving in the bright green jade made even Seth's untrained eyes grow as big as saucers. Bloodred sapphires that sparkled brilliantly in the sun had been used for the eyes of the fierce panther's head.

Seth threw the money bags in the back of the truck and stepped over to take a closer look. "Can we count the money, too?" asked Seth, practically drooling over the treasure.

Josh snapped the box closed and slid the latch back into place. "Not here. We've got to get moving."

Josh placed the teak box into a red gym bag and then hid it under the rest of the loot in the back of the truck. "Tie down the back, then check the oil," he ordered. "I'll wipe down the Caddy for prints. We wouldn't want anyone to know we've been here."

🌵

Mike Fowler did his best thinking when he was alone. As he and Jake made their way down a back alley of town, he reviewed the possible methods by which he might dig up a new case. Perhaps if he stopped by the sheriff's office, Smitty might have a lead. It was a little bit out of his way, but he had the time, and it was worth a shot.

Jake barked, breaking Mike's concentration. Mike still had the ball they had been playing with, and the dog wanted to resume the game. Mike lobbed the ball in a slow arc over some telephone wires. It hit and then bounced off an aluminum trash can.

Jake was gone in a flash and caught the ball in his mouth by the second bounce. Before Mike knew it, Jake was back by his side waiting for another round.

This time Mike thought he would make the game a little more challenging. He threw the ball with all his might and gave it a little backspin, just to throw Jake off. The ball sailed almost fifty yards before it came back down to earth, catching the edge of an old Campbell's alphabet soup can. That, together with the backspin, caused the ball to take a weird bounce. Banking off a stray piece of aluminum siding, the ball made a right turn and sailed just over the top of an old wooden fence. Jake arrived just moments later, but there was no way he could follow it over the tall fence.

"Sorry, Jake!" Mike called. "Hold on! I'll get it!"

Jake stood up, placing his front paws as high as he could on the boards. As Mike ran up, Jake turned to look at him and whined.

"Don't worry, boy," Mike soothed. "We'll find it."

Mike grabbed the top of the fence and swung a leg up. Wedging his sneaker between two of the slats, he hoisted himself up and was about to pull himself over the top when he saw, only about twenty yards away, two men behind the back of an old army truck. Mike froze, not out of fear, but because he immediately sensed that something was not right. Since they had not spotted him yet, he slowly lowered himself back down the alley side of the fence.

"That's weird," he whispered to Jake. "This place is supposed to be closed up."

He stood up on tiptoe, just high enough to see over the fence. A lanky redheaded man wearing a cowboy hat was busy tying down the canvas flaps on the back of the truck. The other man had the physique of a bodybuilder and glanced around suspiciously before walking out of Mike's sight. Mike continued to watch until the redhead had finished the job and walked off in the same direction the other had gone.

Mike knew that he probably shouldn't go sticking his nose into other people's business, but he had already come up with three good reasons to do just that. One: They were strangers. He had never seen them around town before. Two: What business could strangers possibly have in the middle of an old, condemned motor lodge? And three: He just had to see what was in the back of that truck!

"They're up to something," he whispered to Jake. "Come on!"

Mike quickly scaled the fence, being careful not to make too much noise when he landed on the other side. He turned and pulled on a loose board, which swiveled to make an entryway for Jake. Mike put a finger to his mouth, signaling the dog to keep quiet, then peeked around the adobe wall to make sure the coast was clear.

Mike could easily make out the pants of the red-haired man, who had his head and shoulders buried under the hood of the car. And he could hear the bodybuilder making noises on the far end of the courtyard.

Signaling Jake to follow, Mike lightly tiptoed across the open ground, being careful not to scuff his feet. Once he had made it to the back of the truck, he went to work untying the canvas flaps. It wasn't easy. The red-haired man had tied it down pretty well, leaving a mean knot to untangle. Mike tried to make his fingers work quickly as he realized that he didn't have much time before they returned.

Just when he was about to give up, the knot gave, and the flaps swung free. Not wasting any time, Mike placed a foot on the truck's back bumper, spread the canvas flaps back, and stuck his head in.

Mike had suspected the two men were up to some kind of no good, but never did he expect to find all this. Unopened boxes of TVs, VCRs, and car stereos were stacked against the back wall. In the middle of the truck bed, safety-deposit boxes were haphazardly stacked, some of them spilling their contents of assorted jewelry and stacks of savings bonds. A long suitcase lay half open, clearly exposing a twelve-gauge shotgun. And closest to Mike was a pile of money bags, each bearing the official symbol of the Bank of Ambrosia.

Mike shook his head in disbelief. This was bad. Perhaps if he could get to the sheriff's office fast enough, he might be able to return with Smitty before the robbers left town.

He decided not to waste any time tying down the canvas flaps and lightly stepped back off the truck. "C'mon, Jake," he whispered. "We've got to go get Sheriff Smitty."

Thunk! The truck rocked to the sound of the hood being slammed. Mike didn't have much time. He'd have to move quickly if he didn't want to be seen.

Mike peeked around the right side of the truck, and his worst fears were realized. The muscular man had finished whatever he had been up to and was now walking up the right-hand side of the truck. It was too late to go back the way he had come.

Mike pivoted on the ball of his foot and peered around the left side of the truck. The cowboy was coming up that side! With nowhere left to run, Mike knew that within a matter of moments he would be discovered.

❦

As Josh Pendleton walked along the side of the truck, he tried to remember if there was some small detail he might be forgetting, something the police could find and use as a clue. Although he was anxious to clear out of Ambrosia, he knew far too many men back in prison that had panicked, made a sloppy mistake, and been caught because of it. No, he would keep a level head and mind the details.

He came to the back of the truck, turned the corner, and stopped short in his tracks. "Hey!" he yelled at the top of his lungs.

Seth rounded the opposite side of the truck at about the same time. "What?" he asked, wondering what he could have done this time.

The canvas flaps blew loosely in the wind. "I distinctly told you to tie this down!" Josh bellowed, pointing at the flaps.

Seth looked at the untied flaps in disbelief. "I thought I did," he stammered.

"You *thought* you did. Tell you what, I'll do the

thinking. You just do what you're told. OK? Now, tie it down!"

Josh turned and walked back to the front of the truck shaking his head. This was exactly the kind of slipup he was afraid of. He'd have to keep a close eye on his not-so-brilliant partner.

Seth stood for a moment at the back of the truck scratching his head. He was sure he had tied those flaps down, but there was no denying the evidence. The tie-downs just hung there, flapping in the wind. He couldn't let Josh down again. This time he'd use his own extraspecial industrial-strength knot.

It had only been because of some quick thinking and a lot of luck that Mike had not been discovered. With both exits cut off by the robbers, it had occurred to him that he had one last option. He had scooped Jake up in his arms and scrambled through the flaps into the truck.

He was sure he had been seen, especially when one of the robbers had yelled. But he had overheard their conversation and knew that he was safe for the time being. He now hunkered down with Jake behind a large TV box and waited for a chance to slip back out.

From his hiding place he could see the fingers

of the cowboy securely retying the canvas flaps. He heard a door open and felt the truck's weight shift as the other robber climbed into the front. Next came the sound of the tinkling of keys, and then the engine roared to life.

"Are you almost done back there?" the driver yelled back impatiently.

"You asked me to tie it down. So that's what I'm doing!" the other responded defensively.

"Well, hurry up. We haven't got all day!"

Mike could hear the cowboy's footsteps walking up to the front of the truck. This was his chance.

"C'mon, Jake," he whispered to the dog. "We've gotta move quick."

Mike stumbled across the scattered loot, grasped the canvas flaps, and tried to pull them apart. They barely budged. The cowboy had apparently tied them down twice as well this time. Mike tried to reach his fingers through to the knot, but it was no use. There wasn't enough room.

Mike heard the driver grind the manual transmission into first gear and felt the truck start to roll forward. *It's now or never!* Mike thought. Seeing a bit of light seeping through at the top of the flaps, Mike reached up and made a hole. Although it wasn't very big, he hoped it would be large enough to squeeze through. He pushed his right shoulder through the hole and was working on the other one when the truck made a left turn, setting him off balance. His foot landed on Jake's paw, and the dog let out a small yelp of pain.

Mike knew he only had a few moments left. Once the truck pulled out of the driveway onto the main highway, it would pick up too much speed for him to jump away safely.

Mike regained his balance and pushed his other shoulder through. Now, if he could just lift his leg over onto the bumper.

Something at his waist was snagged. It was the compass he kept in a pouch on his waist. He pushed open the canvas as far as it would go, and the compass came free. The truck swerved, and Mike lost his footing again. As he grasped at the flaps to regain his balance, the pouch at his waist snapped open and spilled the compass onto the bumper.

The compass had been a gift from his father. Along with a pocket Bible, it was, in fact, the last thing Mike had ever received from his dad. *I can't lose it!* his brain screamed.

Mike forgot all else and reached as hard as he could for the compass, but it was just out of his reach. The vibration of the truck was slowly moving the compass precariously close to the edge of the bumper. Mike made one last lunge, stretching his arm and fingers as far as they would go.

The truck hit a pothole, and the compass bounced away. With his arm still extended, Mike watched it bounce several times on the blacktop before disappearing into a patch of weeds on the side of the drive.

As the truck pulled out onto the highway and accelerated away from town, Mike realized that it was too late to get away. He and Jake had missed their opportunity and were now trapped.

3

Ben, Winnie, and Spence were growing impatient as they waited inside the B-17. Mike was over an hour late, and it was beginning to grow dark outside.

"I bet he forgot," said Spence, checking his watch.

Winnie paced the floor, a scowl on her face. "You mean Mike—*our* Mike—forget a detective meeting? I don't think so."

"Last time I forgot a meeting you guys made me eat a jar of prunes," Ben complained.

"That's because you were home watching *Saber Force,*" Winnie sharply reminded him.

Ben shrugged and looked to Spence for some sympathy. "It's my favorite show."

Spence didn't want to take sides. He knew that they needed to concentrate on the problem at hand. "OK, guys. Mike would treat this like a case. Fact: Mike doesn't miss meetings. Fact: Mike missed this one. Where else could he be?"

"You guys worry too much," Ben said with a yawn. "He's probably goofing off somewhere with Jake."

As Mike slowly rubbed Jake's head, the dog looked up at him with sad eyes. Somehow even he knew they were in a lot of trouble.

They had been on the road for a few hours, and as far as Mike could tell, they were headed deep into the wastelands of the desert. He had hoped that the robbers might stop for gas, giving him another chance to escape. But no such luck.

"Well, I guess it's time to play Hansel and Gretel again," he whispered to Jake. Mike reached into a money bag lying between his legs and pulled out a one-hundred-dollar bill. He lifted the side of the canvas and let the wind carry it away.

The idea had occurred to him just a few miles outside of town. Since then he had been dropping a few twenties and hundreds every mile or so. Once in a while he would even write a quick note on one with a gold pen he had found in a safety-deposit box. But he knew the chances of someone finding one of them were slim. The desert winds would probably just blow them off the road and cover them with sand.

He had already emptied almost an entire money bag and decided to get another. When he pulled one away from the rest of the pile, he noticed that he had uncovered a red gym bag. Unzipping the bag, he reached his hand in and came up with a small wooden box. Curious, he released the latch and opened it up.

At first Mike didn't quite know what to make of the statuette. But after giving it a closer look, he noticed the finely detailed carving and the inlaid jewels in the head. *This is probably worth a lot,* he guessed.

"Ever see a green cat with wings?" he asked as he showed it to Jake.

Jake's ears went flat and he let out a low growl. He hated cats.

Mike placed the empty box back in the gym bag and slid the statuette into his coat pocket. "We're going to keep this baby as evidence!"

✲

The Last Chance Diner was winding down for the day, and Gail Fowler was glad. She and Grandma had been waiting tables all day, and her feet could use a much earned break. Besides, she looked forward to seeing Pop and Mike. They normally arrived about this time to eat a late supper together as a family.

She was making change at the checkout counter when she heard the bell above the door ring, signaling that yet another customer had arrived. But she was too busy to look up.

"Eight thirty-five's your change," she said to a trucker as she handed him his cash. "Thanks for stopping in."

Winnie, Ben, and Spence approached the counter, glancing around as if looking for something, or someone.

"Hi, kids," Gail called as she closed the drawer on the cash register. She looked up, noticing that there were only three of them. "Where's Mike?"

"He's not here?" Winnie asked in reply.

"No, I haven't seen him since he left to meet up with you guys. Weren't you playing baseball all day?"

"Well, yeah," Ben said awkwardly. "But we finished up hours ago."

"Mike said that he was coming here and that we should meet up with him at five-thirty," Spence added.

Gail glanced at her watch. It was almost quarter after seven. After exchanging a worried glance with the kids, she crossed to the center island, where Grandma Fowler was clearing plates.

"Mom, have you seen Mike today?" Gail asked.

"No, sure haven't," Grandma said, shaking her head.

"Do you know if he's with Pop?"

"Well, no . . ." Grandma noticed the worried expression on Gail's face. "Is there a problem?"

"We don't know where Mike is," Gail said as she gestured at the kids.

"Well, Pop is due back soon—he had to make a run into town." Grandma reached over and grabbed Gail's hand reassuringly. "Oh, they'll probably come walking in the door together in a few minutes."

"I hope you're right," was all Gail could say.

🌵

Josh Pendleton jammed his foot onto the brakes as hard as he could. The tires caught the pavement immediately, and the truck fishtailed to a screeching halt. His partner, Seth, who had just been on the verge of falling asleep, planted his face into the windshield.

"Hey! What's wrong, now?!" Seth asked, rubbing the area where a bump would soon appear on his forehead.

Josh gestured to the side mirror. "I saw something back there."

"Like wha—"

Josh jammed the stick shift into reverse and hit the gas. Seth left another greasy face imprint right next to the other one on the windshield.

Josh backed the truck up almost fifty yards, then jumped out, grabbing a flashlight from under the bench seat on his way. When a bewildered Seth met him around the back of the truck, Josh was busy searching the ground with the flashlight beam.

"What's gotten into you, Josh? There's nothin' back here but road."

"Aha!" Josh exclaimed triumphantly. He bent over something at the side of the road and picked it up.

"What? What is it, Josh?" Seth asked, trying to peer over his shoulder.

Josh paused for a moment as he studied his find in the flashlight beam. Standing up slowly, he turned and held it out for Seth to see.

It was a crisp, new one-hundred-dollar bill. As Seth leaned in for a closer look, he noticed that something had been written on it: "Call Ambrosia Sheriff!—Mike."

Seth didn't quite know what to make of it and looked to Josh for an explanation. "But I don't get it," Seth sputtered.

Josh paused, looking pitifully at Seth for a moment, then turned and walked purposefully to the back of the truck. He grabbed the canvas flaps with both hands and violently threw them open. Seth's eyes slowly followed Josh's flashlight beam to the inside of the truck. There, a young boy and his dog sat blinking in the harsh blue light.

An evil smile grew across Josh's face. "So . . . you must be Mike!"

It was a little after seven-thirty when Pop finally pulled his pale blue pickup to the front of the diner. He had been out at the airstrip all day rebuilding an old Cessna engine and had worked up quite an appetite.

It was Saturday night, and that meant that the blue-plate special was Grandma's fried chicken and biscuits, smothered in a layer of steaming gravy. Pop's mouth watered at the thought.

As he turned off the ignition and pulled the emergency brake into place, he noticed the front door of the diner open. Gail, Grandma, and the kids rushed out to meet him.

"Now, I knew we offered some of the best service in town, but since when did we start valet parking?" Pop joked as he stepped out of the truck.

"Pop, have you seen Mike?" asked Gail, rushing up to meet him.

From the tone of her voice, Pop sensed something was wrong. His eyes quickly scanned the others' faces. Nobody was smiling.

"Uh, no. What's up?"

"He didn't show up for our meeting," Ben said.

"We haven't seen him since before noon," Winnie added.

"Pop, he hasn't called or anything." Gail took a deep breath to calm her emotions. "We were hoping he was with you."

Pop cared very deeply for Mike. Sure, he was his grandfather, but since the plane crash, Pop had had to step in and act more as a father figure. Their relationship had grown very close over the past several years, and especially after Gail and Mike moved to Ambrosia. If there was one thing Pop knew about Mike, it was that he was responsible. True, the boy was always running off in search of another wild adventure—he was like his dad that way—but Mike wouldn't just disappear without telling someone.

"That doesn't sound like Mike," Pop said finally. "Let's go look for him first. Then we'd better call Smitty."

After locking up the diner, Gail and Grandma joined Pop in the cab of the truck. The kids piled into the back.

As Pop pulled onto the interstate, Gail hoped that her worries were unfounded and that Mike would show up with some logical explanation. But in the pit of her stomach, she had a growing sense of dread. She had already lost a husband—she couldn't bear the thought of losing her son as well.

It was going to be a long ride into town.

4

Mike Fowler was in trouble, and he knew it. Armed robbery was a federal offense that carried a lengthy prison sentence. With so much on the line, these men couldn't just let him go.

The one called Josh tied Mike's hands together behind his back and then hog-tied him by wrapping his wrists and feet together. Mike was then roughly returned to the back of the truck for "safekeeping."

As for Jake, Mike had been forced to hold him back when they were captured. Although the dog was full of fight, Mike knew the robbers wouldn't have given a second thought to shooting him on the spot. Jake now lay at Mike's side, a short rope tethering him to an inside brace of the truck.

As the truck droned down the road, Josh sat with his legs crossed just a few feet away from Mike. He was busy going through the money bags, trying to establish how much the boy had tossed out onto the highway. He wasn't in the best of moods, to say the least.

Mike held his breath as Josh reached over and picked up the red gym bag. Luckily, the robber only checked to make sure the teak box was still there; he didn't open it. Mike was tempted to just come right out and tell him that he had taken the statuette and put it in his coat pocket. But he had made it this far without them knowing—maybe he could use it as a bargaining tool later.

Josh finished taking inventory of the bank loot and returned to make sure the knots holding Mike's hands and feet were secure. The boy had been a nuisance. The only real hitch in Josh's plan.

"So, Mikey, I guess you're one of those nosy

types. You know, the kind that can't keep out of other people's business."

"It's what I do," Mike said a little sheepishly. He knew it was going to sound corny, but he went ahead and said it anyway. "I'm a . . . detective."

"Yeah?" Josh responded in mock surprise. "What a coincidence. I'm *Batman!* Robin's driving the truck." Josh began to laugh, tickled at his own joke.

Mike slowly lowered his head. He knew when he was being made fun of. "This is wrong," he finally said. "This money isn't yours."

Josh's laughing stopped. "Oh, Mr. Detective Man is going to tell me about right and wrong now," Josh said with a hint of anger in his voice. "Well, I've got a news flash for ya, Mikey. You made a wrong move snooping around. And I don't like complications."

A shiver ran up and down Mike's spine. The way Josh had said the word *complications* gave Mike a sense of dread, like Josh had a way of dealing with complications.

"Are you going to kill me?" asked Mike, his voice slightly cracking.

"Oh, I'd never do anything like that," Josh said with a hurt look on his face. He grabbed the side of the truck and eased himself to a stooping position.

As Mike looked up at him he could see that his face had changed.

"Not when the desert can do it for me," Josh said with a ghastly grin.

As the weight of those words slowly sank into Mike's mind, Josh banged on the back of the cab with his fist.

"Seth! Pull over!" he yelled.

The truck slowed to a stop on the shoulder of the road, and Josh jumped out. As he tied down the canvas flaps, he took one last look in at Mike and said, "By the way, bright boy, leaving that trail of money was just a waste of *your* time and *my* good cash. If anybody does find one of those bills, I'm willing to bet that they don't tell anyone and just keep it for themselves." He paused for a moment and then added, "But just in case a Good Samaritan does come along . . . well, I think we'd best get off the main road for a while and have ourselves a little off-road adventure!"

Josh chuckled on his way to the cab of the truck. Once he was inside, the truck eased its way back onto the highway.

They had not traveled over ten miles before the truck pulled off onto a lonely dirt road. The only thing that marked the road was a sign: FIRE LAKE WILDERNESS AREA: ENTER AT YOUR OWN RISK!

News of the bank robbery spread fast in Ambrosia. Although the town was too small to have its own local news telecast, by evening the sheriff's office had been swamped with phone calls from inquiring minds. The police dispatcher, Arlene, was doing her best to field the calls, while on the desks behind her, two FBI agents and a state trooper were busy setting up a small command post.

The door to Sheriff Smitty's office was off to one side. The office itself was not very big, but at least it afforded some privacy. Smitty sat at his desk, slowly rubbing his forehead with his index fingers. It had been a long day, and he was working on one whale of a migraine headache. And the fact that Mike Fowler was now missing was only making it worse.

Pop and Kate Fowler were seated across from him. Gail Fowler nervously paced the floor while Winnie, Ben, and Spence looked on.

Smitty closed his eyes, trying to concentrate on one problem at a time. "And you've checked the *whole* town for him?"

"The best we could in the dark," Pop said, leaning forward in his chair.

"Officially, I can't mount a search for him until he's been gone for twenty-four hours." Smitty hated to say that so matter-of-factly. He knew it sounded cold. He had known the Fowlers for years and counted them as friends. But he couldn't just tell the FBI agents waiting outside that he was dropping the bank-robbery investigation to go looking for a missing kid. He had rules and regulations to abide by.

"Look," he said, "maybe I can put out an APB."

Gail stopped in her tracks and gave him an astonished look. "An APB? That's it?"

"I'm sorry, Gail. I'm doing my job. The bank robbery has us absolutely swamped with details."

"Details?" Gail began. "Smitty, Mike never—"

"Gail," Smitty interrupted, "I understand. Believe me, I do. I'd like to know where he is, too."

Gail slowly sat down in one of the chairs. She was close to tears.

"Look, missing persons usually show up on their own. Mike's a smart kid. He'll turn up," Smitty said, trying to reassure them.

"Is there anything else we can do, Smitty?" asked Pop.

"I'm afraid you've done what you can tonight, Pop. You'd best go on home and wait for tomorrow. We'll keep our eyes open for him."

That's it, then, Gail thought. *All we can do is wait.*

An old familiar feeling of dread washed over her. She had waited patiently once before . . . and her husband never was found.

❧

Mike guessed that at least three hours had passed since they left the paved highway. As the truck finally slowed to a stop, he tried to estimate how far they might have come. He had no way of telling, really. Since he had not been able to look out and see plants and bushes go by, it was almost impossible to gauge the speed of the truck. But he had been bounced around a lot. That was for sure. He had plenty of bruises that reminded him of that. So they must have been moving at a pretty fast clip.

As Mike listened to the robbers' footsteps approach the back of the truck, he realized that it didn't really matter how many miles they had traveled. Whether it was one hundred miles or only fifty, it still meant the same thing: They were a long way from any witnesses. The robbers could now do what they wanted with him.

Josh opened the canvas flaps, lowered the tailgate, and hopped into the back of the truck. He untied Mike's feet and motioned for Seth to join him.

"Get the dog," Josh said, pulling Mike toward the tailgate.

Jake let out a low growl as Seth gingerly approached.

"That dog better not cause any trouble," Josh warned Mike.

"It's OK, boy," Mike yelled back to Jake. "Go with him."

Obeying his master, Jake reluctantly allowed Seth to take his lead and followed him out of the truck.

Josh and Seth led their captives around to the front of the truck, where they stood backlit by the headlights.

"End of the line, Mikey boy," Josh said, spinning Mike around to face him.

This is it! thought Mike. *The moment of truth!*

Out of the corner of his eye, Mike saw Josh's hand reach for something in his belt. Although he was afraid to look, Mike forced his eyes to focus on what the robber now held in his hand. *It was a gun!*

Seth saw it, too, and the expression on his face said that he was as surprised as Mike.

"Now, Josh," Seth stammered, dropping Jake's rope and moving forward. "We agreed—"

"Back off!" yelled Josh. "I know what I'm doing!" Josh raised the gun above his head and fired it twice into the air.

It takes hunting dogs months, sometimes years, of practice to get used to the sound of a gun going off. Jake wasn't a hunting dog. At the sound of the shots, he spooked and took off running through the brush as fast as he could.

"Jake!" Mike screamed.

Jake hesitated, wanting to return to his master. But Josh fired another deafening salvo of shots.

"Run, Jake! Run!" yelled Josh. "Watch out for the bobcats!"

Mike watched as Jake ran even faster, finally disappearing into the darkness.

"You didn't have to do that," Seth said, slightly dumbfounded by what had just occurred.

Josh was getting tired of his partner questioning his actions. And he had definitely had enough of the pesky kid. He pulled a knife from his pocket, snapped the blade into place, and held it up for them both to see.

"I don't like complications," he growled.

Josh spun Mike roughly around and quickly cut the rope, releasing his hands. He then walked around Mike, to look at him face-to-face.

"See? I'm a good guy. But now you're gonna find out what all your mighty ideas do for you when there's no one around to wipe your nose." Josh stuck a steely finger into Mike's chest. "You're all alone, hotshot."

Sticking the knife back into his pocket, Josh turned and headed for the truck.

"Tie up the back," he said, motioning for Seth to follow him. "Let's go."

Seth hesitated for a moment. He knew that they had to get rid of the kid. After all, he was the only one who knew what they were driving and in which direction they were headed. But to leave him out in the middle of the desert was like sentencing him to a slow death.

Seth glanced over to make sure Josh wasn't looking. Confident that he was unwatched, Seth reached into his back pocket and pulled out a liter-sized bottle of water. He quickly passed it over to Mike.

"Um, good luck, kid," Seth said with a sympathetic look on his face. He then turned and trotted to the back of the truck.

All Mike could do was stand there and watch as they secured the truck down and then finally drove off into the distance. Mike's eyes followed the retreating red taillights as long as they could. After a while, they were only fleeting pinpoints—and then they were gone.

Then Mike slumped to the ground, realizing the full measure of his situation. He was utterly lost . . . and all alone.

5

The sandstorm hit without warning. It had been almost an hour since the robbers had left, and Mike had spent most of that time shouting as loud as he could for Jake. He was beginning to lose his voice when he thought he heard something. But it turned out to be only the howl of the wind as it announced the coming blizzard of sand.

Mike had heard about sandstorms—how they erased the desert landscape and could blow buildings to the ground. But he wasn't prepared for what he was about to experience.

It hit all at once. The roar of the wind was deafening. Fine particles of sand stung his face like the attack of a million tiny bees. He turned his back to the onslaught and tried to look for cover, but he couldn't see any farther than a foot away. A large gust of wind pushed him to the ground, and it was then that he realized he couldn't breathe!

Each gasp of breath brought thousands of minuscule grains of sand into his lungs. He choked and gagged until he finally discovered that pulling his jacket over his head made the air breathable. He eventually removed his jacket altogether and made a small tent for his head. The only thing he could do was lie on the ground, holding the jacket over his head, and wait for the storm to pass.

When Mike awoke in the morning, he was surprised that he had slept. The last thing that he remembered was thinking that the storm would never end.

He tried to move, but it felt like he was

encased in a large bowl of Jell-O. He discovered that the storm had buried him in almost a foot of sand. He slowly rose out of it, like a mummy from one of those old movies on the Late Late Show.

As the first light of dawn lit up the sky, Mike wiped the sand from his eyes and took in his real first look at his surroundings. As far as the eye could see was just more of the same: a desolate panorama of desert. No tire tracks. No roads. Not a single sign of civilization. And no Jake!

"Jake! . . . Jake! . . . Jaaake!" Mike called, pivoting so he could be heard in all directions. "Jake, where are you?"

Mike stood there for a moment listening for any kind of answer. But none came.

Resigned to the fact that he was all alone, Mike bitterly dropped to his knees and then fell back to a sitting position. After a moment, he realized that it would do no good to just sit and feel sorry for himself. He had to do something constructive.

He decided to take an inventory of what he had on him. Maybe he could discover something that would come in handy later. He dug into his coat pocket, and the first thing he found was the jade statuette.

"Lot of help you'll be," he said, tossing it aside. His hand went to the empty leather pouch that usually held his compass. *Boy, could I use that about now,* he thought.

Next, he reached into his back pocket and pulled out his pocket Bible. He opened it up and began thumbing through its pages.

Looking at it reminded him of his father. He remembered the last time he had ever seen him. His father had carefully wrapped the compass and the pocket Bible together in a box for Mike's birthday. And when he gave it to Mike, he had said, "As long as you keep these with you, your paths will always be straight."

The fluttering of the Bible's pages in the wind brought Mike back to reality. Focusing on the page that it happened to have opened to, his eyes went wide. A verse seemed to pop off the page in front of him. "I will never leave you nor forsake you."

Mike smiled and closed his eyes. "Thank you, Lord," he prayed. "Thank you for being here with me right now! You know what kind of a fix I'm in. Please help me. Amen."

Mike opened his eyes and noticed the water bottle sticking out of his coat pocket. He recognized that God had already been at work. Something had made Seth decide to give the water bottle to him. And Mike knew what that something was—God's provision.

Seeing the water bottle made Mike realize just

how thirsty he was. The sandstorm had lined his mouth and throat with a thin layer of dust, and he could feel the grittiness of the sand between his teeth. He could use a drink about now, he decided, as long as he was careful to ration it for later.

He carefully unscrewed the lid and was in the middle of taking a small swig when he heard it— the distant bark of a dog!

"Jake?" Mike whispered, hardly daring to believe his ears.

Being careful not to spill any of his precious water, he quickly screwed the cap back on and leapt to his feet.

"Jake!" he yelled, cupping his hands together around his mouth.

This time he was sure he heard an answer and turned to look in that direction. At first he saw nothing, and then there was some movement on a distant rise. It was Jake all right. He didn't quite look the same because he was covered with light brown dust, but Mike knew it was Jake.

Seeing his master, Jake raced toward him, still trailing the rope tied to his collar. He never slowed down and then leapt the last five yards, knocking Mike over onto his back.

"Jake!" Mike cried between Jake's happy reunion licks. "Oh, man, I knew you'd come back for me."

The two joyously wrestled around for a few minutes until Mike finally sat back to take a breather. Revitalized, he leaned on one arm, petting the dog, and took stock of the situation. He couldn't fool himself. He was still up a creek without a paddle. He was hopelessly lost and an awfully long way from home.

"OK, now," Mike said, scanning the horizon. "Where's Kansas, Toto?"

He had always heard that if a person was lost, he should stay put right where he was. That way he wouldn't accidentally head off in the wrong direction, giving the would-be rescuers an even larger area to search.

But Mike's father had taught him to use his head. And in a situation like this, he knew he couldn't just sit back and wait for a rescue party to show up. No one could possibly have any idea where he was. And although he was sure they were beginning to look for him at home, he also knew that, with God's help, he would have to pull his own fat out of the fire on this one.

He decided to head due east. Since he didn't know which way civilization lay, it was as good a direction as any, he guessed. He would use the sun as his compass. He would head toward it in the morning, and it would set behind him at dusk.

He decided that before he left he'd better leave

a marker. Gathering rocks, he made a large letter *M* and an arrow pointing east. It was a trick he had picked up from his dad. The letter and arrow were large enough to spot from the air and would tell a pilot which direction he had headed.

When he stepped back to examine his work, he noticed the jade statuette still lying where he had tossed it. He walked over and picked it up. "Who knows," he said, placing it back in his coat pocket. "Maybe we'll make it."

Before he and Jake began their journey, Mike knelt on one knee and said another prayer. But this time he didn't just pray for himself and his own problems. He prayed for his mom, too. He knew that she had been through this once before, and he was sorry to put her through it again.

🌵

Back in Ambrosia, Winnie, Spence, and Ben were trying to do what they could to aid in the search.

First, they had ridden their bikes to the Fowler household. Pop had come out, looking like he had been up all night, and told them that there was still no sign of Mike and that Smitty had not come up with any leads. Next, they rode into town and checked in at the sheriff's office. Arlene told them that Smitty was much too busy to see them, unless they had found some new evidence that might help him out.

And so they decided to do just that—find new evidence. After all, even without Mike, they were still a detective team. Why not see what they could dig up on their own?

They determined that they should start at the bank since that was the last place Mike had been seen. Then they would retrace the path he would have had to take to get home. The only problem was, Mike could have taken several possible routes home. And knowing Mike, he may have thrown in a detour or two.

And so they broke up, each taking a parallel route on separate streets.

After an hour, they met up at the southern edge of town. Spence and Winnie had already met up when Ben came pedaling around the corner, breathing heavily.

"Nothing on Kramer Street," he panted as he pulled his bike next to theirs. "You guys find anything?"

"No," Winnie said in a low voice. "And I don't think he would have come this far."

"Oh," said Ben, sensing their low spirits. "Then I guess there's really nothing else—"

Crash! Winnie let her bike fall to the ground while she walked up a driveway to be by herself.

She didn't want Spence and Ben to see her cry. The two boys stood there in an awkward silence, not sure what to do.

"So," said Ben to Spence, trying to make some small talk. "Can you believe someone knocked off the bank yesterday? We should investigate that case."

Spence didn't say anything. He just handed his canteen to Ben.

"I mean, after we find Mike," Ben quickly added.

Winnie walked to the side of the driveway and wiped the tears from her eyes. She had never cried in front of the others before, but this time she felt so helpless. If only they had some kind of clue to work on. Something to take their minds off their worries. Something that made them feel that they were somehow getting nearer. Something—

She had been kicking at some weeds at the side of the driveway when she saw it. At first, she thought it was just a reflection of an old discarded soda can, but all of a sudden something looked strangely familiar. As she gently parted the weeds, her eyes opened wide in recognition. *Mike's compass!* "Spence! Ben!" cried Winnie.

Dropping their bikes, they raced to her side. With trembling hands, she showed them her find. "He was here!" was all she could manage to say.

Ben's mouth dropped wide open. Spence immediately began to assess the situation. His eyes focused on the letters on an old sign hanging over their heads.

"'Howdy Partner!'" Spence said, reading the sign out loud.

"Howdy," replied Ben, still in shock.

"No. This place. It's called the Howdy Partner! Motor Lodge," said Spence. "But what would Mike be doing here?"

"C'mon." Winnie motioned for the others to follow her as she made her way through a hole in the fence.

Once in the courtyard, they spread out, their eyes scanning for any signs of life.

"Mike?" called Winnie.

"Hey, Mike!" yelled Ben.

They listened quietly, but no response came.

"Maybe he was just passing by," Ben whispered.

"Hey, guys!" Spence yelled. He was crouched near the back of the courtyard, waving for them to come over. "Look at this!"

As they neared him, they could see that he was holding a small red ball in his hands.

"Jake's ball!" Spence exclaimed victoriously.

"He *was* here!" said Ben in awe.

The clues were coming together quickly now. They could feel that they were getting closer with each new find. With renewed vigor they continued their search, scouring the ground and peeking in all the abandoned rooms.

A dirty old tarp covering a large object caught Winnie's attention. As she pulled the canvas back, her face went white. She recognized the Cadillac immediately as the car they had seen in front of the bank.

"Illinois!" she mumbled as she stared at the license plate.

She knew it could only mean one thing: Mike was with the bank robbers!

6

Within an hour, the Howdy Partner! Motor Lodge was a beehive of activity. State and local police cars were parked at odd angles around the property, their red lights strobing against the adobe walls. Yellow police-barrier tape had already been stretched around the perimeter in an attempt to keep local reporters and curious bystanders from disturbing the evidence.

Inside the courtyard, a handful of officers were busy photographing and measuring a fresh set of tire tracks they had found in the dust. At the same time, other officers were going through the motel room by room, searching for anything the robbers might have left behind. The abandoned Cadillac was now the center of attention for two FBI agents. They carefully dusted it for fingerprints and took hair and fiber samples that would later be sent to their lab.

Sheriff Smitty paced back and forth, directing the whole operation. Lack of sleep didn't seem to matter to him anymore. He now had a trail to follow. And like a bloodhound on the hunt, he felt more alert than ever. He walked through the yard barking orders, a look of stubborn determination etched across his face.

"Tom, I want a match on these tire tracks ASAP," he called to a trooper.

Another officer walked up and handed him a hot cup of coffee and a dispatch that had just come in over the wire. Smitty didn't even break his stride, but grabbed them both and continued on his way through the yard.

"Bev, call Search and Rescue. I want someone in the air immediately!" he said after a scalding gulp of coffee.

His eyes scanned the dispatch. It confirmed his

suspicions. Ducking under the yellow barrier tape, he walked to the truck where Pop, Gail, Grandma, and the kids were anxiously waiting.

"Well, we've got a positive ID on the car. It *is* the one used yesterday in the bank robbery," he said. He folded the dispatch and placed it into his back pocket. His face was somber. "I'm afraid it looks like Mike stumbled across the two suspects when they were switching vehicles."

Hearing the news, Gail took a deep painful breath and closed her eyes. It wasn't what she wanted to hear, but at least they knew *something*.

"What do you know about these men, Smitty?" Pop asked.

"We think we know who they are. Two other banks in small towns have been robbed by men matching their descriptions and MO," Smitty explained. "The good news is that they have never once hurt anyone. It's not their style. We're going to get them."

"Smitty," an officer called from behind the barricade.

"Sorry, I've got to go," Smitty said. "I'll let you know when we have more information."

As Smitty eased himself under the yellow tape and walked back into the courtyard of the motel, Pop followed him until they were out of earshot of the others.

"Smitty," Pop called in a somber voice.

Smitty stopped and turned, slightly taken aback.

"Look," Pop said, stepping close to him. "I know you, you know me. Let's put the polite talk aside. Tell me the truth about my grandson."

Smitty took a long, deep breath and then pulled the police dispatch out of his back pocket. Unfolding the paper, he handed it to Pop. Pop quickly glanced over it and then looked to Smitty to explain its meaning.

"I think he's with them, Pop," Smitty explained, shaking his head. "But it doesn't make any sense. These guys aren't the hostage type. They're fast in, fast out. Mike would just slow them down. The truth is, Mike is in a bad situation. There are lots of prettier words, but they don't hide the meaning."

Pop handed the dispatch back to Smitty. There was a slight tremble to his voice. "Smitty, we *can't* lose him."

Smitty just looked back at him. There was really nothing else he could say.

"Smitty!"

The voice surprised both of them. They turned around to discover that Gail had been listening in on their conversation.

"Smitty . . . I . . ." Gail's words faded away as she tried to regain her composure.

Smitty saw the tears welling up in her eyes and realized that she was about to break down. He had to say something. He had to give her some kind of hope.

"Gail, I *will* bring him home!" Smitty said in a determined voice that left little room for doubt. He turned on his heel and walked purposefully back to the command post. He had two men and a boy to find.

Mike knew that the journey across the desert wastelands was going to be tough. He knew that the near future promised incredible hardships that would test the limits of his endurance. But the utter impossibility of the challenge that lay ahead was just beginning to fully dawn on him.

The sun burned mercilessly upon his shoulders and head as he plodded across the searing sand. He stopped for a moment and squinted at the distant hills. He had hoped to make them by noon. But the sun was at its apex, and the hills didn't seem to be getting any closer.

Josh had dropped him off in this area for a reason: He didn't think Mike would be able to make it out alive. Even with the water bottle, Mike knew his chances of making it were slim to none.

Persistence! Mike thought to himself. *That's*

what I need, persistence! Even a snail will eventually make it across the entire distance of a driveway . . . that is, if the sun doesn't fry him first.

Mike knew he had to put the doubt and fear out of his mind. He knew he had to just concentrate on the job at hand. It was his only chance. Tired, Mike knelt on one knee and put his hand on Jake's back. The poor dog's coat was almost too hot to touch. "You OK there, buddy?" he asked Jake.

Jake let out a small whimper and tried to crawl into Mike's shadow.

Mike carefully unscrewed the lid on the water bottle and took a small swig. The water was warm, but it still felt great as it slowly trickled down his throat.

"We have to get out of the sun," Mike groaned, scanning the barren expanse around them.

Jake licked his chops and stared eagerly at the water bottle.

"Don't worry, boy. I didn't forget about you," Mike said.

He slowly poured a small pool of water into his cupped hand. Jake didn't waste any time but quickly lapped it up until Mike's hand was dry.

"I wish I could give you some more," Mike apologized. "But we've got to ration this for later."

Mike shaded his eyes and took one last look around. Except for a few football-sized volcanic rocks and some low-lying desert brush, there was no shade to be found anywhere.

Mike stood to his feet and started forward. "C'mon, Jake. There's gotta be an umbrella out there somewhere."

The Last Chance Diner and Gas Station had been open every Monday through Saturday as far back as most people in Ambrosia could remember. But not today. A signboard that swung lazily in the warm breeze read, Sorry, We're Closed.

Inside, Pop, Grandma, Gail, and the three kids sat together in one of the larger booths. They had locked the entrance and closed the blinds to ensure their privacy.

"There must be something we can do," Winnie lamented, looking vacantly into an empty water glass.

"Yeah, but I'm afraid it's pretty tough without a trail, Winnie," Pop said. "We may have to wait for them to be spotted somewhere or to spend some of those large bills they stole from the bank."

"Yeah," Ben added. "Then we could track 'em down before they hurt Mike."

65

Gail winced at the thought of Mike being harmed by the kidnappers. Ben was a master at sticking his foot in his mouth, and Winnie shot him a dirty look for making such an insensitive remark in front of Mike's mom.

"What?" he asked, not realizing what he had said.

Winnie tried to discreetly point in Gail's direction. Ben suddenly got the message and regretfully hung his head.

"It's OK, Ben," Gail said. "If I just didn't feel so . . . helpless."

"Sometimes that's when the good Lord does his best work," Grandma reminded them.

"Well, I'll sure welcome any help the good Lord sends our way," sighed Gail.

Tap, tap, tap. There was a knock at the front door.

"We're closed!" hollered Grandma to the door.

Tap, tap, tap. The knocking persisted.

"I'll get it," Winnie said, rising and walking to the door. Winnie peaked through the blinds and recognized a scarecrow of a man called Harley Fisher.

Everyone in Ambrosia knew of the eccentric old desert rat. His skinny frame was a common sight along the roads around town. He daily made his rounds up and down the interstate, searching for lost hubcaps and aluminum cans. He had a face that reminded people of an old cracked leather saddle. And he smelled like he hadn't taken a bath since last Christmas.

Winnie turned the key in the lock and opened the door just wide enough to be heard but not enough to let the smell in. "Hi, um, the diner's closed," Winnie apologized through the crack in the door.

"Are you kiddin'?" boomed Harley. "On a day of miracles like this? 'For the Lord said unto Moses, Behold, I will rain bread from heaven for you.'"

"Huh?" said Winnie, not catching his drift.

Harley held up a crisp one-hundred-dollar bill and snapped it open for her to see.

"One hundred dollars!" he exclaimed, beaming from ear to ear. "Found it out on the highway."

The old man was so happy, it seemed like he might begin dancing a jig at any moment. "Certainly you can find *something* in the kitchen to—"

Before he could finish what he was saying, several pairs of hands reached out and yanked him into the diner.

This was the break they had all been waiting for, and they weren't about to let it get away.

🌵

It had taken the better part of a day, but Mike and Jake had finally made it to the hills they had seen in the distance—only they weren't typical hills. They were sand dunes.

67

The creation of a sand dune is a strange phenomenon. The high winds that blow across the desert pick up the very smallest particles of sand and carry them aloft. Once the winds hit an area where they are forced to die down, the particles drop out of the sky and are deposited on the desert floor. Day after day, month after month, year after year, this goes on until large white piles of sand, or dunes, are created. They never stop growing; they are always expanding in height and width.

Mike knew that if he was going to continue on his present course, he would have to go over the dunes. To detour around them would take much too long. And the way he was using up his water meant he didn't have time not to take any shortcut he could. So he set about climbing the shifting hills.

After he had been at it for over an hour, he began to wonder if it had been such a good idea. The sand cruelly reflected the sun into his face like it was bouncing off a mirror. With each step his foot sank into the fine sand up to his ankle. He felt like he was walking through wet concrete with sandbags tied to each foot. His breathing was labored, and his shirt was drenched with sweat.

He decided to stop for a moment. He could not keep up at this pace without a rest. He pulled out his water bottle once again to share it with Jake. When it was his turn, he had to resist the temptation to just guzzle it all down.

He looked up at the crest of the dune. He had already climbed almost halfway there. He estimated that the top was another four hundred feet. The problem was that he had no idea what was on the other side. He hoped that once he reached the top he would be able to descend back to the desert floor, but he feared that he might just find more mountains of sand.

A low growl caught his attention. At first he thought it was Jake, but then he realized that it was his own stomach making the noise. It had been over twenty-four hours since he had last eaten. Yesterday morning, he had shared a sandwich with Spence at the baseball game. He wondered how long someone could go without food. He guessed that it didn't really matter. If he ran out of water, he wouldn't last a full day.

He checked his water bottle. It was already half empty. "C'mon, Jake," Mike said, standing up on his shaky legs. "We've had all the rest we can afford for now."

Mike took a couple steps, forcing his tired legs forward. He suddenly realized that he had stood up too fast. The heat and his own exhaustion were making him light headed. For a moment he thought that he might pass out. He stuck out an arm to balance himself but lost his footing in the deep sand. He landed on his side and started tumbling out of control down the hill. Arms flailing, he rolled almost fifteen yards before he was able to bring himself to a stop.

He shook his head to get the sand out of his face and looked around to see if Jake was all right. The dog was still standing where Mike had left him, intently staring at a spot on the ground between him and Mike.

As Mike followed Jake's gaze, his eyes went wide. It was the water bottle! It had fallen out of his pocket during the fall, and he must have rolled over it. The plastic side was cracked and caved in, water spilling out of the split.

"No!" yelled Mike.

Forgetting about his tired legs, he dug his toes into the sand and started to scramble back up the hill. He had to get there before it was too late!

Time seemed to slow to a snail's pace. As he pushed his legs as fast as they would go, his eyes watched the water bottle continue to spill its precious contents into the desert sand. Mike dove the last couple yards and grabbed the bottle in his right hand. But it was too late. He watched as the last drop of water fell and disappeared into the all-consuming sand.

For a moment he looked at the ground in disbelief. *No! This isn't happening!*

He dropped the empty water bottle and dug frantically into the sand, hoping that somehow he might be able to create a puddle from which to drink. But it was all in vain. The water was gone.

His arms slowed their digging as the futility of what he was trying to do slowly sank in. He rolled over onto his back in bitter resignation and covered his face with his forearms.

"Noooooo!" Mike screamed at the sun.

He knew that the desert would not forgive him his mistake. Without water, he may as well have been handed a death sentence.

7

Tom, pull my truck around. I think we've got a lead!" Smitty ordered. He reached over and pulled his hat off a nearby coatrack. "Arlene, call Andy Anders over at the bank. Tell him to meet me out at the Last Chance Diner, pronto!"

Smitty felt like a bloodhound on a hot trail. Although he was confident that the robbers would eventually be brought to justice, he knew that time was of the essence. The longer Mike was missing, the worse his chances of survival were.

When Smitty and Tom pulled up to the Last Chance Diner, Andy Anders was already waiting for them. The bank manager looked a little out of place standing in the dirt parking lot in his three-piece suit. A tumbleweed made a beeline for him and snagged itself on his pant leg. He tried to kick it loose, but it hung on like a stubborn pit bull. He finally reached down in an attempt to unhook it and caught a thorn in his finger for his trouble.

"Hey, Andy," Smitty called as he climbed out of the truck. "Would you be able to identify a bill from the robbery if you saw it?"

"Shouldn't be a problem," said Andy, sucking on his bleeding finger. "For the most part, they were consecutively numbered."

"Good!" Smitty said. "There's something I want you to see."

Andy followed Smitty and Tom into the diner. Part of the tumbleweed was still attached to his leg.

As they entered, all three noticed Harley sitting wide eyed at the diner's counter. A silly smile was stretched across his face. Before him sat a spread of food that was fit for a king.

"Where is it, Pop?" asked Smitty, wasting no time.

Pop pulled the hundred-dollar bill from his pocket and handed it to Smitty. "Right here."

In turn, Smitty passed it on to the bank manager. "Well? Is it one of yours?"

Andy carefully took the bill and walked up to one of the windows where he could see it more clearly. They all held their breath and waited for his answer.

"Yes! No doubt about it," Andy finally said. He spun on his wing-tip shoes to face the others. "The numbers match. It's definitely one of ours."

Smitty gave Pop a congratulatory slap on the back and then slid onto a stool next to Harley. He pulled out a pad of paper to take notes on. "So, where exactly did you find it, Harley?"

Harley was busy eyeballing a piece of boysenberry pie Grandma Fowler had just placed in front of him.

"Uh, you got a couple more of those?" Harley asked through a mouthful of biscuits.

"Sure," replied Kate, amazed that someone so thin could put away so much food.

"And how about some ice cream on the top?" added Harley.

"Look," interrupted Smitty, "we've got a very pressing situation here—"

"Out on 102, Sheriff. West of town," explained Harley, spraying Smitty with biscuit crumbs.

"There he was, old Ben Franklin staring up at me, pretty as you please."

Smitty gestured for his deputy. "Tom, get on the horn. They're headed west." Tom quickly exited the diner and went to the radio in the sheriff's truck outside.

Pop set his hands on the counter and looked across at Smitty. "Well, at least we've got something to go on. Any hunches, Smitty?"

"L.A., Vegas, maybe some shack in the hills," Smitty said, letting out a deep sigh. "I dunno, Pop."

Smitty flipped the pages of his notepad and mentally reviewed the clues. Winnie, Ben, and Spence approached from behind him.

"We want to help, Sheriff," Winnie said, a note of intensity in her voice. "Maybe Mike left a trail."

Smitty didn't look up from his pad of paper. "I appreciate your wanting to help, Winnie, but, uh . . ."

He could feel three pairs of eyes trained on his back. He set the notepad on the counter and swiveled on the stool to face the three kids. They looked like three soldiers just waiting for their marching orders. They were all business.

They did find Mike's compass at the motor lodge, Smitty thought. *And it's not like they've been getting in the way. Besides, they're Mike's best friends.*

"How could I say no?" Smitty finally said. "Listen, I've got an idea. . . ."

🌵

Mike knew that he had to keep going. Even though it seemed like an impossible task without water, it was better than just giving up and being eventually swallowed up by the sand dunes. If that happened, his fate would forever become just another mystery. For his mom's sake he had to try to make it back.

He finally managed to reach the top of the sand crest he had been climbing. From that vantage he got a good look at what lay ahead. The good news was that once he made it down the other side, the sand dunes came to an end. The bad news was that all they had been hiding were miles of desolate desert that went on as far as the eye could see.

Getting to the bottom was pretty easy. All he had to do was sit down and push. He slid down the dunes as easily as sledding down a mountain of snow. The only difference was that the sand radiated temperatures exceeding 140 degrees.

Once they made it to the flat desert floor, Mike noticed that Jake was limping. He realized that the sand must have burned Jake's tender paws. His own neck and face were already burned from prolonged exposure to the sun. He was afraid of what he would look like at the end of the day. But that was the least of his worries.

They continued on, mile after aching mile. Mike didn't know if they were getting closer to or heading farther away from civilization. He could feel each minute he spent in the sun slowly sapping him of his strength.

After what seemed like endless hours of walking, he finally topped a rise and paused for a moment. He still had a few more hours of sunlight left, but he felt too worn out, hungry, and thirsty to continue on. With his head hanging, he fell to his knees and slowly drew the back of his hand across his parched lips. Jake let out a pitiful whimper at his side.

"Sorry, Jake," Mike weakly whispered. "I just gotta rest for a—"

Something caught Mike's eye. It was just a familiar shape at first. But after squinting his bleary eyes, he was able to make it come into focus.

"What?" Mike said, slowly rising to his feet.

A plane sat only forty-five yards ahead. It was only a small, orange-and-white two-seater, but it was a plane nevertheless.

Hanging around with Pop at the airfield had given Mike an informal education about airplanes. He could tell the make and model of most by sight. As he drew closer to the craft, he recognized that it was a Cessna 186, or what was left of one.

The prop blades were twisted back crazily. One wing was almost sheared off. The tail was bent to one side, exposing a wicked tear in the back of the plane. It had obviously crash-landed. And from the looks of it, the plane had been baking in the desert for quite a few years.

Just another casualty of the desert, Mike thought.

At first he felt sorry for the pilot, but as he looked over the wreckage and saw no sign of dried blood, he guessed that there had been no casualties. The pilot had probably radioed his position before going down and was picked up within a few short hours.

Mike wished that it could be that easy for him. Although he was sure that search parties were looking for him, how could they possibly know he was this far from home?

He slid through the gaping hole in the side of the airplane and made his way to the cockpit. The seats had been stripped of their cushions, probably by desert mice trying to insulate their nests.

Mike sat on the rusted springs of the pilot's seat and examined the instrument panel. Surprisingly, the gauges were all still intact. Mike guessed that the wreck was too deep in the desert for anyone to be interested in salvaging it. He flipped on all the switches, on the outside chance that the radio might still work—but the batteries had long since died.

Giving up, he searched the entire airplane, going through all of its small compartments and looking under the scattered debris on the floor. But in the end he came up with nothing that would come in handy.

When Mike finally exited the airplane, he found Jake lying in the cool shade of the wing.

"Well, Jake," Mike said, looking down at the dog. "We're not flying out of here."

Jake managed a few weak barks in reply.

"Yeah, I know how you feel," Mike said with a sigh. "I'm all tuckered out, too. If nothing else, this plane gives off some pretty good shade. And if a sandstorm should blow in tonight, we can just climb inside for shelter. I vote we bed down here for the night."

Jake seemed to understand and barked his approval.

Reaching down to pet the dog, Mike noticed a nylon strap half-buried in the sand. He reached over and tried to pick it up, but it was anchored to something below the surface. Mike knelt down and started to scoop the sand away. Once he had dug a foot below the surface, Mike discovered that the strap was secured to a bright orange barrel-shaped plastic container.

Pulling it free from the sand, Mike inspected the container until he found that it was made up of two halves that screwed together. Twisting both halves, Mike easily opened the container and carefully poured out its contents onto the ground. Mike couldn't believe his eyes when he saw what was inside. Before him lay a flare gun, six unused flare cartridges, an instruction booklet, and a box of safety matches. Mike picked up the gun and held it in his hands in disbelief.

"Jake!" Mike exclaimed excitedly. "This is our ticket home!"

8

Smitty's plan as to how the kids might help the investigation was not only simple, it also made a lot of sense. He had a hunch that the hundred-dollar bill Harley had found was not the only one out there. If he knew Mike like he thought he did, then the kid just might have managed to leave some sort of trail.

He was already shorthanded back in town,

which left the job up to him to do. He knew his vision wasn't what it used to be, so he decided to let the kids do the eye straining for him. Together they would be able to cover at least three times the territory he could by himself. Smitty asked the kids to go get their quad runners and meet him out on the highway. Once they had gathered at the spot where Harley had found the bill, Smitty had the kids spread out a few yards away from each other. Their job was to slowly make their way down the highway and scour the brush on the shoulder for any remaining clues. Smitty followed in his police pickup, the light bar flashing, warning any motorists to slow down and make way.

Within an hour, they found three more hundred-dollar bills, each about a mile apart. Although it was exciting to be on the trail, Smitty knew they would never be able to catch up to the robbers at their current snail's pace.

Smitty looked out through his windshield and studied the horizon. It would be getting dark in an hour or so. Soon he would have to call off the search for the day.

Spence pulled his quad into a sharp U-turn and peered at a bush he had just passed.

"Hey! Over here!" Spence called. He climbed off his quad runner and, kneeling on all fours, reached under a small pile of tumbleweeds. He pulled out another bill and waved it triumphantly over his head for the others to see.

"Great work, Spence!" Ben yelled. "That makes five!"

As Spence took a closer look at the bill, his face registered a look of surprise. "Wait a minute! Guys! Come here, quick!"

Winnie and Ben turned their quads around and headed to Spence's position. He ran up to meet them and excitedly handed the bill to Winnie. "Look!" Spence exclaimed, pointing at the bill.

Ben craned his neck over Winnie's shoulder to get a look. "Whoa!" was all he could say.

Smitty pulled the truck up alongside them. "What have you got there?" he asked.

Winnie handed the bill through the window and simply said, "Mike!"

At first Smitty saw nothing uncommon about the bill. But flipping it over he found that a hand-written message had been quickly scribbled on the back. It read, "Army truck. M."

🌵

As the afternoon temperatures started to cool, Mike lay with Jake, resting in the shadow of the abandoned plane. With his head propped against its aluminum side, he watched the sun slowly begin to sink behind a desert mesa.

It was the first time that day he had allowed his body to really relax. As he lay there breathing deeply, he noticed that the grumbling in his stomach was turning into outright hunger pangs.

He had to find something to eat soon. But where?

Thinking back on all the miles they had covered that day, he could not remember seeing another living thing—aside from an occasional sand fly buzzing by—out in the dunes. He closed his eyes and decided that he would worry about finding a source of food the next day.

It was then that he heard it.

The sound seemed to be coming from inside the airplane. It was a slight brushing sound—not like a twig in the wind, but like something that was slowly moving about. He quietly got to his feet and looked into the airplane cabin. Everything was just as he had left it, and no movement caught his eye. He waited and listened until he heard it again.

This time he circled the aircraft, searching all of its outer walls for any signs of life. He had almost completed his circle and was nearing the tail of the plane when he saw a small cloud of dust rise from under the base of the plane.

He quietly knelt down to see where the dust was coming from and discovered a small six-inch-wide hole. It was obviously an entrance to some kind of lair under the airplane. Something had found a safe haven from the sun and was moving around down there—maybe even coming out now that it was cooling off.

Jake came walking around the corner to see what was up. Mike put his finger to his lips. "Shhh." He motioned for Jake to follow him, and they hid behind a small rise.

Mike had wanted food, and maybe this was the answer. As much as he didn't like the idea of eating a prairie-dog burger, he knew that he had to assume that this might be the last opportunity he would get to eat anything.

After a few minutes his patience paid off. At first only a snout was visible. Then the mouth opened to allow a long black tongue to taste the air. And then it crept forward, its entire body coming into view.

It was the biggest, scaliest lizard Mike had ever seen. From nose to tail it had to be over two feet long. It paused for a moment, cautiously looking around, and then slowly crawled away from the plane.

Mike had seen a few Gila monsters in the desert before. They were brightly marked with orange-and-black spots and had a terribly poisonous bite. This, however, was no Gila monster. It was slate gray with large, dime-sized scales.

He and Jake followed the lizard at a distance. Either they were not seen, or the lizard didn't care that it was being watched. It finally crawled up onto a large rock to sun itself in the last rays of the day.

Mike hated to have to kill any living creature, but if he planned to survive, he didn't have much of a choice.

He had read stories of plane crash survivors eating bugs and snails and other disgusting things to survive. With that in mind, he didn't think lizard meat would be all that bad. Besides, it would probably just taste like chicken.

Mike snuck up behind the lizard. He found a large rock and decided it would make an appropriate weapon. But in his weakened state, Mike's throw missed his target by a mile. The lizard gave him a disgusted look and slowly scampered away.

Mike told Jake to keep an eye on the lizard while he went to find a more suitable weapon. Returning to the airplane, Mike fashioned a crude spear out of some loose parts. A jagged piece of aluminum made up the head of the spear, and the shaft was a three-foot metal rod. It was all tied together with one of Mike's own shoestrings. It wasn't much to look at, but it would do the job.

After several valiant attempts, Mike realized

that he wasn't a javelin thrower either. Each of his throws fell either far short or wide of the lizard. The sun would be going down soon, which meant that he didn't have much time left and would have to abandon the subtle approach.

Mike slowly inched forward on his belly until he was within target range. He suddenly sprang to his feet and charged forward—kamikaze style—the spear held high in both hands over his head.

"Yaaaaa!" he screamed, plunging the spear downward with all his might.

🌵

By nightfall, Mike had the lizard cleaned and roasting on an open spit over a campfire. Lying on his side, he tossed a small twig onto the embers and playfully ruffled Jake's fur.

"You ever been camping, Jake?" Mike asked, staring deeply into the flames. "It's great."

Mike thought back to the warm memory of his last camping experience. It had been several months before the "accident." His father had taken him up high into the mountains for a father-son weekend away. They had sat around a fire, just like the one he now stared into, cooking their dinner in the clear mountain air.

"Somehow, the food just tastes better," Mike

said in reflection. "And the water—man, it's so clear . . . and cold. . . ."

His voice trailed off as more memories came flooding back. Mike remembered the camping trip as if it had only happened yesterday. It was as if he could almost hear the babbling of a clear mountain stream.

He and his father had stood side by side, idly chatting as they fished from the bank. Mike had been lucky enough to get the first bite. And it was a big one! His fishing pole had bent as if were about to break under the great weight of the thrashing trout. It was all Mike could do to just hang on to it.

His dad jumped around excitedly and shouted his encouragement. "C'mon! Stay with it, Son!"

"Uh, Dad, maybe you'd better—" Mike gestured for his dad to take the pole.

"No way! This is *your* battle, Mike. Don't give up now! You can do it! . . . There you go! Just like I taught you. . . . Ease back on the pole, then reel in some line."

Mike smiled as he remembered his dad's enthusiastic coaching. It was always his father's loving encouragement that pushed him beyond what he thought were his limits. Now that he was older, Mike realized that his father had been constantly teaching him lessons about life, as if he knew their time together was limited.

Mike wondered how his father might advise him in his present situation. Suddenly, another old memory materialized in his mind.

It was the same day they had gone fishing. Only now it was night, and Mike lay alongside his dad, enjoying the warmth of his own sleeping bag. As Mike gazed up at the countless stars, his dad read a psalm as a closing devotional before they fell asleep.

"'The Lord is my shepherd,'" he began, "'I shall not be in want. He makes me lie down in green pastures, he leads me beside quiet waters, he restores my soul. He guides me in paths of righteousness for his name's sake. Even though I walk through the valley of the shadow of death, I will fear no evil, for you are with me.'"

A loud crack from the campfire brought Mike back to the present. But the words his father had read from the Bible still echoed in his head. "For you are with me," Mike slowly repeated, taking comfort in each word.

Jake whined and cast an eager eye at the sizzling lizard meat.

"Oh, all right," Mike said, reaching for the stick that held it over the fire. "It ought to be well done by now."

Mike held the smoking, charred remains in front of him by both ends of the skewer. He took a careful sniff and involuntarily shuddered. Even though his stomach's aches were getting worse, he wondered if he actually could go through with it.

He looked toward heaven to offer a prayer. "Lord, for this—" he could barely bring himself to say the word—"meal . . . I give you thanks. Amen."

Mike swallowed hard and gave the meat one last inspection.

"It still looks like a lizard, Jake!" he complained. "I wonder what the people back home would do if they ordered a hamburger and it came out still looking like a cow?"

Jake tilted his head to one side and licked his chops.

"All right, you try it!" Mike tore off a hind leg and tossed it to Jake. "But don't expect much of a bone to chew on."

Jake carefully sniffed at the meat for a moment and then began eating. Within a couple of seconds, he had polished off his portion and was looking to Mike for more.

"So, it meets your approval, does it?" Mike pulled the meat up close to his mouth. "Now, I guess it's my turn."

Mike closed his eyes and tried to think of chicken. He decided he'd better do it quick, rather than think about it too long. He quickly bit down hard and tore off a large chunk. His eyes steadily watered as his mouth chewed on the rubbery meat.

"Well, it doesn't taste quite like chicken," he noted between shudders. "Tastes more like burnt lizard. But I guess under the circumstances, it'll have to do."

Although he didn't enjoy one bite, Mike forced himself to eat until he was full. He knew that he'd need every ounce of strength he could muster to make it through the next day. Especially now that he was without water.

He went to sleep that night hanging all of his hopes on the flare gun that he had found. *Maybe tomorrow I can signal a plane!*

9

Mike and Jake slept soundly that night under the wing of the airplane. They both needed the rest badly after what they had been through the day before. And luckily no sandstorm ever materialized to disturb them.

Mike slept so peacefully that he even had a dream. Just like his present situation, he was lost in the desert. Only this time, his father came and found him, and he flew Mike and Jake home in his F-15. It was a warm, happy dream that made Mike smile even as he slept.

As the first rays of dawn slowly crept across the desert, a familiar noise made Mike stir from his deep sleep. He slowly opened his eyes and tried to identify what he was hearing. It was a kind of low, droning noise, like a distant . . . *plane!*

Mike's eyes popped open, and he scrambled to his feet. He ran out from under the wing and frantically searched the sky for the source of the sound.

It took him a few moments, but he finally spotted it. Just above the northern horizon a small plane was floating along the rim of a distant peak.

Mike raced back to the airplane, shouting to Jake. "It's an airplane, Jake! I think it's a search plane! *Our* search plane!"

Mike's hands fumbled as he tried to open the orange canister. He finally unscrewed the two halves and dumped the contents to the ground. He quickly grabbed the flare gun and turned to run, but then remembered that he needed the flare cartridges. He raced back in a minor panic and snatched a handful of flares. Then he ran back into the open, attempting to load the gun on the way. Jake followed after him barking excitedly.

"Come on. Come on!" he mumbled, trying to load a flare into the chamber. It slipped from his hand and fell to the ground. As he reached down to pick it up, he stole a quick glance at the distant search plane. It was headed away.

Slamming the flare into the chamber, Mike snapped the breech closed and raised the gun high into the air. Squinting his eyes and turning his face away from the muzzle, he slowly squeezed the trigger until the hammer fell.

What he expected to hear was a large explosion, followed by a *whoosh* as the flare rocketed away. But the only noise that met his ears was a small disappointing *poof,* followed by a slight fizzling sound.

Mike continued to hold the gun in the air, expecting something more to happen. When it didn't, he slowly lowered the pistol and examined the barrel. A pitiful wisp of smoke slowly floated into the air.

"It was a dud!" he said in bitter disbelief. "A lousy dud!" He threw the gun to the ground and fell to his knees in defeat. In the distance he could hear the last hums of the plane as it faded away.

He tilted his head back, looked to the sky, and shouted a plea: "I could use a little help down here!"

Jake slowly approached his master and nuzzled him with his nose.

"It's OK, Jake. Maybe another will come along close enough to spot us," Mike said, trying to bolster both their spirits. "In the meantime, we've got to keep moving and find some water."

🌵

Josh poured himself a tall, cool glass of water and offered Seth a toast. "Hey, amigo! Here's to the completion of another successful business venture!"

"Here, here," answered Seth, raising his own glass.

The two robbers had made it home to Las Vegas and now stood amidst their stolen goods in a warehouse they had rented. It was big enough to back the truck into and offered seclusion from prying eyes. Once they had all the loot tallied they would bring in a professional fence, someone who would sell it all off on the black market for a small but substantial fee.

Josh walked between the unloaded boxes, admiring his handiwork. "Not too shabby, Seth. Especially for our first time out."

"How much did we get?" asked Seth, dangling his feet off the back of the truck.

"Five grand and some change. About what

you'd expect from a Podunk bank, but we'll get fifty times that for the statue." Josh gestured for Seth to hand him the gym bag. "Let's have another look at that little darlin'."

"What's it made out of, solid gold?" Seth said, throwing the bag over to him.

"Uh-uh, jade." Josh reached in and pulled out the teak box. "Some famous sculptor carved it. Collectors are nuts about it because of its history. And now it's going to make us rich." Josh ran his hands slowly over the smooth grain of the wood and then gently unhooked the latch. "Come to Papa!"

When he opened the box, Josh's mouth dropped open, and he let out an audible gasp as if he were in some kind of pain.

"What is it?" asked Seth, sensing that something was terribly wrong.

Josh held the empty box open for Seth to see, and his face twisted in rage. "The kid!" he screamed.

🌵

By noon, Mike could already feel his strength steadily draining away. He knew that it was the lack of water getting to him. Living in the desert, Mike had quickly learned to always bring an ample supply of water along when venturing out. Although under normal conditions the human body could survive for sometimes over a week without water, in the desert's burning heat, a person could become dehydrated within a matter of hours.

The last time he even had a taste of water was nearly twenty-four hours ago. And with each passing hour the merciless sun continued to extract its deadly toll.

A dull headache was growing more intense, and Mike found it harder to focus his thoughts as the day wore on. His eyes felt like dry, scratchy marbles in his head, and his tongue became bone dry. His lips were cracked and swollen. Large sun blisters that he had earned the previous day peppered his bright red face and were growing worse.

"Wait'll Mom sees me." Mike started to smile, but it made the cracks in his lips widen. "Won't I be a sight for sore eyes."

Mike forced his legs forward. He still carried the orange canister from the plane. His jacket was tied loosely around his waist.

He knew he had to take his mind off his misery, or it would get the best of him. He tried quizzing himself aloud on baseball trivia he had picked up. "Longest game ever: twenty-six innings; Boston Braves, Brooklyn Dodgers; 1920. Uh, best lifetime ERA . . ."

Jake faithfully limped along beside him, his tongue hanging out of his mouth, his head hanging low.

Mike picked up a pebble and put it in his mouth. It was an old Indian trick that he had once read about in a book. He remembered that if someone sucked on the pebble, it would cause him to salivate and help stave off his thirst. It worked for an hour or so, but pretty soon his mouth dried up again, and he spit the pebble back out of his mouth.

The desert before them was a sea of flickering waves of heat. Mike felt like a living gingerbread man in the world's biggest oven. He didn't know how much more of this he could take. But for the time being, he had to push on. He had no other choice.

Smitty and Pop stood on the shoulder of the road studying maps of the region that they had laid on the tailgate of Smitty's truck. They had followed the money trail as far as it would take them. Now that it had come to an end, they were trying to figure out what it all meant.

"Smitty. What does your police sense tell you? I mean, have you got any hunches?" Pop asked.

Smitty paused and wiped the back of his neck with a bandana. His shirt was showing large sweat stains from the unrelenting heat. "My guess is that they didn't know they had Mike with them," he began. "Otherwise, how else would he have access to the money bags? Since the trail seems to end here, then he must have been discovered. And that leaves us with two possibilities."

"Which are?" Pop was almost afraid to hear the answer.

"Either they took him with them, which would serve no purpose, or they got rid of him out here somewhere."

"Got rid of him? But Mike would have made it to a town by now if they just dropped him off. Unless . . ." Pop couldn't help but face the possibility he had been trying to drive out of his mind for the past two days. *Mike might have been killed.*

Smitty saw the look on Pop's face and tried to dismiss his fears. "Pop, from the little we know about these guys, they're not murderers. Look, I know it's like grasping at straws, but maybe they dropped him off somewhere where he couldn't—"

Smitty was interrupted by a call on his police radio. "Sheriff Smitty? This is County Search and Rescue. Do you copy?" a voice asked through a field of static.

"Smitty here."

As Pop waited for Smitty to finish, he noticed Spence, Winnie, and Ben returning on their quads.

"Affirmative, Charlie. Keep working the north ridge. We're covering the plateau from Fire Lake

Junction. Smitty out." Smitty tossed the handset onto the seat and walked back to the rear of his truck just as the kids pulled up. "See anything?" he asked them.

"Nope, same as before," Spence explained. "The trail seems to end around here."

Smitty pushed his hat back on his head and went back to studying the maps. "Where is he?" he said to no one in particular.

"If it's all the same, Smitty, we'd like to go look on our own," Winnie suggested. "There's a dirt road up ahead that looks worth exploring. I mean, if that's OK."

Smitty looked to Pop for his opinion. Pop thought it over for a moment and then nodded his approval.

"OK," Smitty said, pointing a finger at them. "But I don't want to have to come looking for you, too. Stay together and report back every twenty minutes on your walkie-talkies. You hear me?"

"Yes, sir. We will," Spence said, patting his radio.

Winnie took the lead for the others to follow. "C'mon!" she yelled, heading out into the desert.

Spence and Ben peeled out eagerly after her, leaving Smitty and Pop in a cloud of dust.

"Every twenty minutes!" Smitty called out after them.

10

Mike tried to push his body to keep on going, but it was past the point of fatigue and was starting to fail him. He stumbled along, his breathing labored and raspy. His tongue was swollen and felt foreign in his mouth. It was all he could do just to keep his feet under him.

He tried to focus his eyes on what lay ahead. A steep, foreboding hill loomed before him. Just a few days ago he could have run to the top of it without being winded. Now it seemed as impossible to climb as Mount Everest. He knew that there was no way he could make it to the top; there was no way he could possibly find the strength. His reserves were all tapped out. But he had to try.

He concentrated on putting one foot in front of the other. The rest of his focus was aimed at just keeping his balance. He had come to the grim realization that if and when he fell, he wouldn't be getting back up.

The words of Psalm 23 came drifting back to him. "'The Lord is . . . my shepherd,'" he haltingly slurred, "'I shall not . . . be in want. . . . He makes me . . . lie down . . . in green . . . pastures—'"

Mike's world began to spin. The colors of the desert seemed to dim and turn to shades of gray. Before he even realized that he was falling, he had hit the ground like a felled tree. He lay flat on his face where he had fallen, not moving. Jake crawled over and curled up next to him. Even he knew what this meant.

Within a few minutes Mike regained a state of semiconsciousness. He was aware that he had been trying to do something—something he had left unfinished—but he couldn't remember what.

Then he remembered the psalm. He had been quoting the psalm. Something told him that he had to finish it. "'Though . . . I walk . . . through the valley . . . of the shadow of . . . death,'" he mumbled, "'I will fear . . . no evil . . . for you . . . are with me.'"

After he completed these words, Mike was filled with a warm inner peace. The tenseness in his muscles slowly began to relax, and his eyelids slipped closed.

"Mike!" He knew the distant voice immediately. It was his dad's! *"C'mon, stay with it, Son. This is your battle, Mike."*

"I tried, Dad. . . . I really tried," Mike managed to hoarsely whisper out loud.

"Don't give up now! You can do it! Stay with it, Son! Ease back on the pole, then reel in some line."

"But it's so hard."

Jake crawled forward at the sound of Mike's voice. He whimpered a few times and then nudged Mike with his nose.

"Camping is . . . great, Jake," Mike said with a weak smile on his face. "You oughta . . . try it sometime."

His thoughts floated back to the camping trip. They were in sleeping bags around the campfire again. His dad was just finishing up the Twenty-third Psalm.

"'. . . and I will dwell in the house of the Lord forever.'" His father closed the Bible and looked reflectively into the fire. "This is a great psalm. It tells us that *God* will be our strength." His dad paused for a moment and looked into Mike's young eyes. "I won't always be there for you, Mike, but God will."

Jake's barking brought Mike back to reality. Somehow he felt strangely refreshed, his spirit had found new courage. "I've got to . . . get up, Jake," Mike said with conviction. "Got to get off the ground and—"

It slowly dawned on Mike that he was already off the ground. In fact, he was standing! "I'm up. . . . I'm up?" He didn't know how he had gotten that way, but he wasn't going to waste time figuring it out. He was just thankful he wasn't still lying there dying. "OK . . . great. . . . We're movin'."

Mike began trudging forward up the steep incline. Somehow he had found, or been given, a second wind. He shook his head in wonder and let out a slight laugh. He was still alive and moving. And it felt good.

"Kinda like the tortoise and the hare. You ever hear that story, Jake? We're two tortoises—*torti*. And this hill is *ours!*"

It took Mike all of ten minutes to scale the back side of the hill. The whole way he kept his mind busy telling Jake the story "The Tortoise and the Hare." The tale was just winding to a close when they finally reached the summit. "So the hare jumps up and races for the finish line. But he was too late because the tortoise never—" Mike stopped in his tracks and got a strange look on his face—"he never gave up." The words escaped over his lips.

He was now standing at the edge of a cliff that overlooked a valley. And the sight of what was in it took Mike's breath away.

It was a town! No more than half a mile away! From his vantage on the cliff he could actually see cars driving around on the streets. And pools! Big, blue backyard pools just bursting with sparkling water!

It's too good to be true, he told himself. *It can't be real. It's gotta be some kind of crazy mirage!* He closed his eyes tightly and then slowly opened them again, afraid that it would all be gone. But it was still there.

"Yes! Ha-ha! We're back!" he cried. "Do you see it, Jake? Do you see it?"

Jake happily barked his reply.

Overcome with emotion, Mike knelt beside his dog and wrapped his arms around him in a huge bear hug. Burying his face deep in Jake's fur, he laughed uncontrollably and wept tears of joy.

Finally releasing his hold, he stood to his feet and pulled the jade statuette out of his pocket. He triumphantly thrust it into the air, like a victorious athlete holding high his hard-won trophy. "Mike is back, and he's got evidence!" he yelled for the world to hear. "You don't mess with the Last Chance Detectives!"

🌵

Mike made his way slowly down the rocky cliff face. He had come too far and fought too hard to allow a careless slip to ruin things now. He followed small varmint trails that zigzagged their way across the sandstone face. It wasn't the shortest way down, but it was definitely the safest. Sometimes the trails were several feet wide; sometimes they disappeared altogether, and Mike had to make things up for a while. But as long as he was making progress, he was satisfied. With the finish line just in front of him, he felt reenergized.

"I'm gonna drink sixteen gallons of water," Mike fantasized out loud. "Then I want five hamburgers—no, cheeseburgers—great big juicy cheeseburgers with extra pickles and a mountain of secret sauce, five chocolate shakes, and a banana split—"

He started to stumble but regained his footing. He decided that he'd better rest for a moment and not let his enthusiasm get the best of him.

"Let's take a breather, Jake," Mike said over his shoulder. "The town can wait a few more minutes—it's not going anywhere."

He steadied himself on a large boulder and then carefully sat down beside it on a foot-wide ledge. Jake sat down beside him, a happy look on his face. With his feet dangling over the edge, Mike leaned slowly over to see what was below. The cliff fell off another sixty feet. Large jagged rocks and dark chasms where the rock had broken away from the cliff waited menacingly down below. "Well, we're not going down that way," he said with a newfound respect.

Mike set the statuette he had been carrying beside him near the boulder and untied his leather jacket that had been secured to his waist. He didn't want it to get snagged on an outcropping and cause him to lose his balance. Even though it was hot, it would be safer to wear it the rest of the way down.

"I wonder what town it is?" he asked, gazing at the town in the distance and savoring the sight. "Could be Cottonwood. I just didn't figure that we were that far south." Mike slipped his arms through the sleeves of his jacket, then hefted it over his shoulders. "I guess it doesn't really matter. As long as it's a town with water, that's good enough for me."

Mike craned his head around to steal a glance at Jake. The dog looked as eager as Mike felt to get off the cliff face and into the town. "All right, if you're ready, I am," Mike said reaching for the statuette at his side. "Just think, within the hour we oughta be—"

Whhiiiirrrrrr.

The sound was unmistakable. Living in the desert, Mike had heard it before. But never this close. It was the deadly whir of a diamondback rattlesnake.

Mike immediately froze his position, his arm still outstretched for the statuette. The fur on the back of Jake's neck stood on end, and the dog let out a low growl.

Keeping his head absolutely still, Mike slowly panned his eyes to his left. There, inches from the statuette under the cool shade of the boulder, Mike could easily make out the distinct black-and-white diamond-patterned rattlesnake. Its five-foot-long body was coiled; its spear-shaped head poised ready to strike. Mike knew that the average rattlesnake could easily strike over half its length. His hand wavered less than a foot away.

Jake's low growling erupted into vicious barking.

"Easy, Jake!" Mike whispered. "Don't make him mad."

As he sat there frozen, like a statue, large beads of sweat dripped down his forehead, stinging as they made their way into his eyes. He didn't dare brush them away.

Mike noticed that his hand was beginning to shake badly. No matter how hard he tried, in his weakened condition, he just couldn't keep his hand still. He thought about yanking it quickly out of the way before the shaking could get any worse. But the thought occurred to him too late.

The snake struck out with such speed that it was only a blur of motion. It sank its razor-sharp teeth deep into Mike's hand and unloaded its deadly payload of venom.

Without thinking, Mike instinctively recoiled away. The movement caused him to lose his seating on the rock, and he began sliding over the side. Panicked, Mike rolled over onto his stomach and dug his fingers into the rock. The fingernail on his index finger tore away as he tried to find a handhold. But he just couldn't make himself stop.

Time seemed to decelerate into slow motion. One moment he was staring up at Jake; the next, he was slowly falling away into empty space.

With a sickening crunch his leg hit a rock outcropping. The impact started him tumbling head over heels. Every few feet he would make contact and then bounce off the sandstone wall.

Mike lost consciousness after being slammed hard one last time against the cliff face. His body bounced clear of the rocks and then disappeared into the inky darkness of a gaping chasm.

After a few seconds, all was silent.

11

It had been over two hours since Ben, Spence, and Winnie had left Pop and Smitty on the side of the road. On the quad runners they were able to cover a lot of miles quickly, and now they were deep in the desert. But they still hadn't found anything.

Spence was taking his turn leading the pack. Ben and Winnie noticed him put on the brakes and come to a stop.

"See something?" asked Ben as he and Winnie pulled up beside Spence.

"No," replied Spence, "but it's been twenty minutes since our last report to Smitty." He pulled the walkie-talkie from the basket on the back of his quad. "Sheriff Smitty . . . this is Spence. Do you copy? Over."

"Go ahead, Spence. This is Smitty," came the reply.

"Just checking in, Smitty. Over."

"You kids see anything?"

"No, sir. Not yet. Over."

There was a long pause before Smitty spoke again. "Listen, you kids better be heading on back now. Over."

"What!" exclaimed Winnie. "Here, hand me that!" Spence passed her the walkie-talkie. "Sheriff Smitty, this is Winnie. What do you mean 'head back'? There's still several hours of light left."

"That's my point. You kids have been gone for almost three hours. It'll take you at least that long to find your way back out to the road again. Over."

"But, Smitty, I've got this feeling that we're getting close," pleaded Winnie. "Just let us go a little bit farther. We've got headlights on the quads. We can turn them on if it gets dark before we get back. Over."

"No, Winnie. It's too risky. We'll never find Mike if we have to go looking for you three, too." Smitty's voice softened. "Listen, you kids have done a great job. We couldn't have gotten this far without your help. Now, head back and meet us where you left us on the highway. Smitty out."

Winnie silently handed Spence the walkie-talkie and then walked away from the quad runners. She had to be alone for a moment. It seemed like it was all becoming so hopeless—she knew how deadly the desert could be.

She remembered an incident that had happened when she was a little girl. Some sightseers had ventured off road to enjoy the desert's beauty, and their car broke down. They hadn't planned on being gone for long and foolishly hadn't brought any water. They only lasted a little more than a day. They were finally found only a few miles from their truck under a cloud of circling buzzards. There wasn't much left for the rescuers to bring back.

Winnie closed her eyes hard and fought back the tears. *I can't allow that to happen to Mike!*

Back at the quad runners, Spence offered Ben a bottle of water. "Better drink up," Spence warned. "You don't want to become dehydrated."

"No, thanks," Ben replied. "I've been drinking so much already, I feel like my eyeballs are going to float away." Ben glanced around at the land-scape around them. "Speaking of which, you think there's a place around here to make a pit stop?"

Spence swung an open hand to a stand of bushes on a nearby hill. "Help yourself."

Ben climbed off his quad and started up the hill. Once he had made it to the top, he pushed his way through the bushes until he had made it to the other side. Now standing in a clearing, he caught a glimpse of something down the opposite side of the hill that just didn't seem to fit in with the surroundings. He did a double take, his eyes widening.

It was a stone marker in the shape of a large let-ter *M*. Only Ben had approached it from the wrong side.

"*W?*" he gasped.

🌵

Smitty and Pop were not as deep in the desert as the kids were, because Smitty's four-wheel drive could not move as fast over the rugged terrain as the kids' quad runners could. Still they figured that they were roughly on a parallel course with the kids and were now heading back to the highway.

The walkie-talkie on the bench seat between Smitty and Pop suddenly blared to life. "Sheriff

Smitty! Come in, Sheriff Smitty!" It was Winnie, and she sounded excited.

Smitty reached over and picked up the walkie-talkie. "Smitty here. What's up, Winnie?"

"I think we've found Mike!"

"You what?!" Smitty slammed his foot on the brakes. "Whaddya mean, you *think?*"

"He was here!"

They could hear Ben's excited voice in the background. "Tell him about the big stone *W*—I mean *M!*"

"He left a marker," Winnie continued. "He's on foot, and we think we know which way he headed. Over."

"Where are you, Winnie?" asked Smitty.

"I think we're about five miles south of you. We can see your dust trail in the distance from here."

"Talk me in, Winnie," Smitty said, patting Pop on the shoulder. "We're on our way!"

🌵

Jake slowly navigated his way down the cliff face, stopping occasionally to stick his nose in the air to try to catch the scent of his master.

Jake had taken care of the rattlesnake—without being bitten. As it tried to slither away, it had exposed part of its midsection. Jake had grabbed it in his mouth and violently thrashed his head back and forth. The swinging momentum kept the rattlesnake from being able to coil, and its head was slowly crushed with each successive blow against the rocks. Jake had made sure that it paid dearly for what it had done to Mike.

Once he was at the base of the cliff, Jake followed his nose until it led him into a narrow crevice. Inside, the fissure opened roughly ten or twelve feet wide, creating a sort of open-ceilinged chamber. It ran almost thirty feet long, until the walls slowly merged back together. The floor was flat and made up mostly of sand. A few sticks and some dead shrubs were scattered here and there.

Though it was dark, Jake could make out Mike's motionless figure lying in the center of the chamber, faintly lit by the reflected light above. Jake ran to his side and gently licked his face, but there was no response. Jake waited a second, let out a whine, and began pushing at Mike with his paw.

Mike took a sudden breath of air as he regained consciousness. He slowly rolled over and let out a groan.

Jake barked happily, glad the boy was still alive.

"Jake?" Mike muttered. He blinked his eyes and tried to make things come into focus. "Where are we?"

Mike had not yet caught his bearings. He tried to think back to what had happened. *That's right, I was climbing! I must have taken a fall!*

Mike managed to slowly raise himself up until he was in a sitting position against the chamber wall. He looked down his body, trying to assess the damage. He had some minor scrapes and bruises. He could feel a large knot still swelling up on the back of his head. He ran his hands down his right leg and was hit by a jolting stab of pain. He guessed his leg was probably broken.

"Well, I'm done climbing today," he told Jake through gritted teeth.

He then noticed something on the back of his hand. On first inspection he had missed it, but looking closer now, he noticed two oozing puncture wounds on the fleshy part of his hand between the thumb and forefinger.

The memory came rushing back. *A rattlesnake! I was bitten by a rattlesnake!* "All right, let's not panic," he told himself out loud. "I've got to keep still. The poison'll spread faster if I don't keep still."

Mike had to think fast, because it wouldn't be long before the poison would begin taking effect. In his already fragile state, he knew he didn't have much time before he would succumb to it.

He grabbed for the flare gun canister that had

fallen a few feet away. He unscrewed the two halves and emptied the contents out into the sand. Knocking the flares off the instruction booklet, Mike grasped the paper in his hand and reached into his pocket for the gold pen he had found in the truck. He quickly scratched a note on the back of the booklet that read, "SNAKE BITE, NEED HELP, FOLLOW DOG."

Working fast, Mike tore off the page he had just written on and tucked it into Jake's collar. "Go into town and get help, Jake," he instructed the dog.

Jake barked in response and then ran in a big circle, finally ending up back at Mike's side.

"Go, Jake. Go!" Mike said louder, gesturing with his arms. "Go into town and bring back help."

Jake barked as if he finally understood and then raced away.

Mike watched until Jake's shadow had disappeared off the crevice wall. "Attaboy, Jake," whispered Mike, his voice growing weaker. "We need help."

🌵

It had taken most of the day for Josh and Seth to retrace the long miles back to Fire Lake. They now drove off-road across the dusty desert in a red four-by-four they had rented back in Las

Vegas. It had been a long, quiet trip. Josh had been stewing the whole way there. Seth had been afraid to say anything lest it set him off.

"Do you think we'll be able to find him again?" asked Seth, finally breaking the silence.

"It's too early to tell," Josh said with a scowl. "But without any water, he shouldn't have gotten too far."

Seth swallowed hard and looked out the window. *If Josh finds out I gave the kid a bottle of water, he'll really blow his stack!*

🌵

With his ears lying flat, Jake ran as fast as his legs would carry him. He could see the town in the distance. Another quarter of a mile and he would be there.

Suddenly Jake came to a sliding stop. His ears had picked up the sound of a vehicle approaching. He saw the dust trail first, and then a truck drove out from behind an outcropping of rocks. Jake looked at the town and then back at the truck. The truck was closer. If he could get the truck to stop, it could get Mike to safety faster.

Jake ran down to the dirt road the truck was traveling on just in time to intercept it. The truck fishtailed to a stop and then slowly backed up to where he stood.

Jake barked as loud as he could and ran up to the door. When the door finally opened, a hand reached out as if to take the message and then grabbed Jake roughly by the collar.

"Hiya, pooch!" Josh said, grinning from ear to ear. Before Jake could break free, Josh snatched the note from under his collar. Jake snapped at him with a ferocious bark. Josh dropped his hold on the collar, and Jake ran free.

"Aw, isn't this nice?" Josh said, examining the paper. "Mikey wrote us a note."

"Why'd you let the dog go?" asked Seth. "Maybe he'd show us where the kid is."

"You kiddin'? That dog hates us." Josh looked out the window at Jake's deep paw prints in the dirt. "We'll follow his tracks. C'mon." Josh handed the note to Seth, slipped the truck into gear, and started backtracking along Jake's trail.

🌵

The sun was already starting to set when Smitty, Pop, and the kids discovered the wrecked Cessna. They found it almost thirty miles due east of Mike's arrow.

Smitty stuck his fingers into the blackened earth where Mike had built his fire. It was still slightly warm. "No doubt about it," he reported to the others. "Looks like he spent the night here."

While the kids picked over the wreckage, Pop searched the perimeter around the airplane. Seeing something at his feet, he reached over and picked up the spent flare cartridge. "Looks like he tried to set off some kind of flare," Pop shouted to the others.

They were becoming more excited with each new find. It was all starting to fall together, and they could sense that they were getting close. Now it was just a matter of time.

"Hey!" Ben popped his head over the side of the wreck. "Come here and check *this* out!"

The others ran over and joined him on the far side of the plane. Ben pointed with a smile at the wall of the baggage compartment. On it a charcoal note had been scribbled in big letters. It was Mike's own handwriting, and it read, "MIKE'S BAR-B-QUE HEAVEN—ASK ABOUT OUR SPECIAL!"

"That's my Mike!" Pop chuckled. "Thank the Lord he still hasn't lost his sense of humor!"

As the minutes slowly ticked by, Mike could feel himself slipping over the edge toward unconsciousness. He was starting to suffer from hallucinations and was having a hard time keeping his eyes from rolling back into his head.

He was afraid of letting himself close his eyes. Afraid that if he passed out, he might never wake up again. He was beginning to have muscle cramps and shake involuntarily from the chills as the venom made its way deeper into his system. "Cold . . . so very cold," he muttered.

He had managed to collect a few dry sticks and twigs that lay around him and now carefully arranged them into a small pile by his side. He opened the box of safety matches and felt inside to discover that only one was left. He held it up in front of his face to examine it, but it was just a blur.

He would get only one shot at it. He knew that he couldn't blow it.

He laid the match head against the cover and quickly pulled it across the rough surface. Nothing happened. He tried it again and this time the match flared to life. With trembling hands he carefully set the flame into the pile of sticks. Slowly, it smoked and then caught fire.

Mike rolled over and waited for the fire to give off its heat. It was then that he heard a noise. He lifted his head and looked toward the entrance of the crevice, but all he could make out were the movements of a blurry shape.

"Jake?" Mike called.

There was no answer.

Mike continued to try to focus his eyes as the shape approached. Suddenly a smile spread across his face. It was his dad!

"Dad, I . . . I knew you'd come," Mike said, extending a hand toward the approaching figure.

"Hello, kid!" his dad said, warmly smiling down at him. "Did you miss me?"

"Oh, Father! You'll never know—" Mike suddenly stopped himself.

The vision in front of him was starting to shift. Mike struggled to bring it back into focus. When he finally did, the face was closer. Only it wasn't the face of his father.

"I'm back!" Josh hissed through a toothy grin.

12

P op, Smitty, and the kids had momentarily stopped their vehicles to take stock of the situation. They had continued traveling due east from the crash site and now were coming up on the small town of Cottonwood.

While the others took turns drinking water out of a large jug, Spence stood in the bed of Smitty's truck and studied the surrounding landscape through a pair of large binoculars.

"Well, I'm beginning to think he may have made it into Cottonwood," said Smitty, gazing off at the buildings in the distance.

"Then maybe we should go look for him there," Ben suggested.

"I'm for that," Pop agreed.

Spence hopped back down off the bed of the truck and handed the binoculars to Smitty.

"See anything, Spence?" Pop asked.

"No," Spence said with a shrug. "Just a red truck over by the cliffs."

"Yeah?" Smitty raised the binoculars in the direction of the truck. "Probably part of the search party. Let's check it out on our way into town."

🌵

Seth stepped around Josh toward Mike and pulled out a canteen to offer him some water.

"Hey! What do you think you're doing?" Josh pushed Seth away.

"Offering him some water! Look at him! He's about ready to die on us."

"Not until we get what we came for!" Josh turned his attention back to Mike and studied his face. "You know, you really should've used a better sunscreen," Josh said, sadly shaking his head.

Using all the strength he could muster, Mike

pulled the flare gun out of his jacket and weakly trained it on Josh. "Go away," he warned.

With one slap with the back of his hand, Josh easily knocked the gun out of Mike's hand. It tumbled away and landed out of Mike's reach.

"Oh, we will. We will," Josh assured him. "But first, I believe you have something that belongs to us. It's about a foot high—and green."

Mike looked off into the distance for a moment, and then a look of recognition came over his face. "Gumby?" he deadpanned.

The veins in Josh's neck and forehead bulged. It looked like he was going to lose it at any second. He finally reined his temper in and turned to Seth, shaking his head. "Can you believe this kid?"

"Uh . . . Gumby's blue," Seth corrected.

For a moment, Josh just stared at Seth, unbelieving. "Not another word!" he finally erupted, pointed a threatening finger at Seth. "Just start looking around. It's got to be here somewhere."

Leaving Mike alone for the time being, the two robbers spread out and started searching the chamber.

Josh returned shortly with an armload of dry sticks. He stoked Mike's small fire until it was a substantial blaze. The dark nooks and crannies of the chamber slowly became illuminated in its light.

Seth crept toward the far end of the crevice

examining the floor. He noticed a thin stream of sunlight hitting the sand at his feet. Curious, he got down on his hands and knees to investigate. Looking through a small narrow crack he was able to see out to where they had parked their truck. His eyes popped at the sight. "Hey, there's a cop and a bunch of kids looking at our truck!" he exclaimed in a low, but panicked voice.

Mike took a deep breath and started to scream, "Smi—"

Josh's hand clamped down over Mike's mouth like a steel trap.

While the kids sat waiting on their quad runners, Smitty walked up to the truck and, after peering in, tried the door handles. They were locked. He looked down at the dirt and noticed two sets of footprints leading away.

"Nothing here to go on," he called back to the others. He glanced up at the rocky cliff. "Maybe they're up there looking around."

Smitty cupped his hands to his mouth and shouted toward the cliffs. "Hello! Can anyone hear me?"

He waited a few seconds, but there was no response.

"Mike!" Winnie called as loud as she could.

They listened again, but only heard the echo of Winnie's voice bouncing back off the rocks. "It's gonna be dark in a few minutes," Winnie said with a worried look on her face.

Smitty walked over and put a comforting hand on her shoulder. "We'll find him," Smitty assured her. "Let's go check in town."

🌵

The inside of the crevice was deathly quiet. Josh and Seth both held their breath as they waited for the people outside to leave. They had heard the voices calling as clear as day, but they weren't about to answer.

If they only knew, Josh thought with a smile on his face.

"Seth, put out the fire!" Josh whispered, finally breaking the silence in the chamber. "I don't want them to get lucky and see a smoke trail."

"OK, but I think they're leaving," Seth whispered back.

Mike knew that if he was going to make a play it had better be now! He looked around, frantically trying to come up with an idea. He spotted the half-buried flare cartridges still lying in the sand where he had dumped them earlier. *If I can only reach them!*

Seth was still lying on his stomach, watching

the people move around outside. "Yeah, look, they're getting in—"

"Put out the fire!" Josh sternly repeated.

"Whatever you say." As Seth rose from his position and started slowly making his way toward the fire, they heard the sound of engines starting.

Josh slowly began relaxing his hold on Mike.

Mike saw his opportunity and took it. He lunged forward and scooped up the flares in his hand. In a move of desperation, Mike aimed as best he could and threw them all toward the red-hot center of the fire. He was lucky—they landed where he'd planned.

Seth had just been ready to stomp his foot into the middle of the fire when it happened. He froze in his tracks as he realized what Mike had done.

Josh jumped to his feet, shielding his eyes from the impending explosion.

But nothing happened.

Seth slowly opened one eye and carefully peered down into the flames. Aside from a little extra smoke, everything looked normal. It looked like the flares were just going to burn themselves out quietly.

Josh and Seth looked at each other with relief and laughed nervously.

Mike lowered his head in bitter defeat. *These signal flares were duds, too!*

"Nice move, bright boy," Josh remarked. He

leaned close to whisper in Mike's ear. "Too bad it didn't work."

As Seth placed his foot back into the fire to stomp it out, the first flare went off with a concussive *bawoom!*

Blinded by the incredibly white light, Josh jerked his head back just in time. A flare rocketed away, just grazing his cheek.

Bawoom! Bawoom! Bawoom! Bawoom! Bawoom! The remaining rockets ignited in rapid succession. Within the tiny chamber, the sound was deafening. The flares flew in all directions, ricocheting off the walls in a shower of sparks.

Mike pulled his leather jacket over his head and lay as flat as he could against the floor. Josh and Seth both ran around in circles looking for cover, their eyes wide in panicked terror. They waved their arms around wildly as if they were trying to swat away a swarm of mad yellow jackets.

The chamber had become a brightly colored conflagration of smoke and whining missiles.

🌵

A few of the missiles managed to find their way free of the chamber and rocketed out of the crevice into the sky. They arced high in the air and then exploded when they had reached their zenith. They bathed the entire desert landscape in a brilliant red light.

Smitty brought his truck to a screeching halt. He jumped out of the door and looked up at the sky in stunned amazement. It looked like some kind of insane Fourth of July extravaganza.

"What in the blue blazes!" he slowly muttered.

"That's gotta be Mike!" Ben said with a knowing smile.

Josh screamed as he saw a flare coming straight for his head. It seared a neat path across his scalp and then bounced off the wall and headed straight back for him.

He turned to run and came face-to-face with Seth. Their heads hit together like a couple of overripe melons, and they fell together to the floor.

They looked up just in time to see that another flare was headed straight for them. They rolled apart, and it hit between them, embedding itself deep in the sandy floor. Then the timed fuse went off, and the rocket exploded. It sent sand flying, turning the larger pebbles into flying shrapnel, which tore through Josh's and Seth's clothes and stung their skin like buckshot. They grabbed themselves and howled in pain.

The smoke seemed to part for a slight moment, and Josh and Seth both caught a glimpse of the exit out of the crevice. It was every man for himself as they scratched and clawed their way out. With flares still chasing them from behind, they finally stumbled clear of the crevice wall and dove headfirst down a shale slope. They finally came skidding to a dusty stop at a pair of large cowboy boots.

As they lay there coughing and sputtering, they slowly became aware that they were lying at someone's feet. They both tilted their heads and followed the legs up until they came face-to-face with the business end of a Smith & Wesson .44 Magnum.

"You boys have a permit for all this?" Smitty said dryly.

Now that things seemed to be under control, Winnie, Ben, and Spence ran past Smitty and entered the smoky crevice. Although all the flares were now out, the place was still thick with smoke.

"Mike? Mike?" Winnie called.

"Over there!" Ben yelled, pointing at a still shape on the floor.

As they raced over to him, Mike slowly pulled the jacket off his head.

"Oh, Mike!" Winnie exclaimed, horrified at his condition.

A smile came slowly to Mike's lips as he looked up at his friends. "Hey, guys," he said weakly. "You ever eat a lizard?"

Epilogue

When Mike entered the hospital, he was in critical condition. The doctors moved fast, filling Mike full of IVs and giving him a shot of rattlesnake serum. Within a couple of hours he had stabilized and had already begun to feel much better.

His right leg had only suffered a slight fracture, but the break was still bad enough that his leg needed a cast. By the time they had finished wrapping it, Mike was fast asleep. That night he slept deeper than he ever had before. And by morning his condition was so improved that he was even allowed to see visitors.

Gail, Pop, Grandma, Winnie, Ben, and Spence all crowded around his hospital bed trying to talk at the same time. Mike looked up at them warmly and drank it all in.

Ben was in the middle of enthusiastically telling the whole story from his point of view. "Your compass was just lying there, so we went into the courtyard of the motel. And Spence said, 'Look at this,' and he held up Jake's ball. And then, when I saw the Illinois license plate, man, I knew you were dead meat!"

Gail Fowler winced at the phrase "dead meat."

Winnie gave Ben a swift elbow to the ribs. "What?" exclaimed Ben, having no clue that he'd done it again.

Gail took advantage of the lull in the conversation and sat down next to her son on the bed. "Mike, while you were . . . missing, I started digging around in some old photos." She pulled a gift-wrapped square package from behind her back. "I had this one framed."

"Thanks, Mom," said Mike as he started unwrapping the picture. "This is great."

The door flew open, and Smitty bounded into the room. He held an empty leash in his hand and had a look on his face like he had just gotten away with something.

"Smuggled a visitor in for ya, Mike," Smitty whispered. "Don't tell the nurse."

Before Mike knew it, Jake had leapt up onto the bed and was in his arms. Except for some bandages wrapped around his feet, he looked like his good old self.

"Jake!" Mike gave him a big hug. "You missed the fireworks show!"

"Hey, everybody! How about a picture?" Grandma suggested. She held up an old antique camera and motioned for everyone to gather around Mike.

As they each jockeyed for position, Mike finished unwrapping the picture his mom had given him. It had been taken during the camping trip. He and his dad stood next to each other, holding fishing poles and grinning from ear to ear. Mike had one hand around the neck of his father. In the other, he proudly held the large trout that he had caught.